Two for Survival

ALSO BY ARTHUR ROTH

The Iceberg Hermit
Snowbound

Weekly Reader Children's Book Club presents

Two for Survival

—— A NOVEL ——

by Arthur Roth

CHARLES SCRIBNER'S SONS   NEW YORK

Copyright © 1976 Arthur J. Roth

Library of Congress Cataloging in Publication Data
Roth, Arthur J   1925–
  Two for survival.
  SUMMARY: Two boys from different backgrounds are
brought together as they try to reach help after sur-
viving a plane crash in the Canadian mountains.
  [1. Adventure stories.   2. Survival—Fiction]
I. Title.
PZ7.R727Tw   [Fic]   76-13632
ISBN 0-684-14721-1

PRINTED IN THE UNITED STATES OF AMERICA
Weekly Reader Children's Book Club Edition

For Alexis Brie Vetrecin, who has given so much joy to her aunt, Arlene Curry.

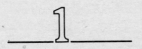

1

John Jenkins leaned back in his seat and stretched out his long legs. A smile crossed his dark, good-looking features as he admitted to himself that so far, knock wood, he was enjoying the plane flight.

At that moment the aircraft hit an air pocket and bumped. John felt his stomach do a flip-flop. He sat up and nervously ran a hand through his short black curly hair. There were three or four quick bumps in a row, as though the aircraft were lurching along the runway on two flat tires. In actual fact the plane had been airborne a good fifteen minutes.

His seat companion, Mark Talbot, grinned and said, "C.A.T."

"Spells 'cat,' " John answered. "You want to try me on 'dog' next?"

"No. C.A.T. means *clear air turbulence*. That's what just happened to us, those bumps."

"I see." John took a long look at Mark's face and smiled to himself. The dudes back on 122nd Street wouldn't believe his seat partner. True-blue eyes, blond hair, pointy little nose, big pink ears, and a "look ma, no-cavities smile"—a real Straight Arrow! He turned to the other two teenagers who sat across the aisle: Annie Hopson and Desmond Corrigan. "Oh man," he thought, "I *am* surrounded!"

The four young people were all high school seniors on their way back from Livingstone College in Maine where they had been weekend guests of the school. All four had applied for scholarships and gone to the college to be interviewed by its scholarship committee. They had not known each other before their visit. En route to Boston, they were now on their way home: John and Desmond to New York City, Mark Talbot to Syracuse, and Annie Hopson to a village at the end of Long Island.

John let his gaze wander over the interior of the aircraft. The plane was less than quarter-full. In the very back row sat three middle-aged men who seemed to know each other but who had hardly exchanged a word since the plane left the runway. In the seat immediately in front of the trio sat a rather old man who, despite his soldierly appearance, gave the impression of being fragile. While there was something military in that erect posture, that neatly clipped moustache, those short sideburns, it was belied by finely drawn pale skin and by intense blue eyes that seemed unnaturally bright, especially in one so old. At the moment the old man seemed to be lost in a world of his own, staring straight ahead.

John turned his attention once again to the young couple across the aisle and eavesdropped on their conversation. Annie, her head bent, was whispering to Desmond, "Do you see the three men behind us?"

Desmond nodded.

"I bet they're sky marshals. You know. Guards to stop skyjacking."

"Naw," Desmond said. "I don't think they have sky marshals on a small airline like this. Anyway they wouldn't put three of them on just one plane."

The aircraft hit another bump and gave a quick, barely noticeable kick.

John Jenkins shifted in his seat and reached for the copy of *Time* in the back pocket of the seat ahead of him. As he opened the magazine, a shadow fell across the page and he looked up. A man's hand was gripping the back of the seat in front of him. The jacket sleeve was pulled back a couple of inches and John momentarily caught a glimpse of a curious red welt, a sort of burn mark, around the man's wrist. He looked up at the face but caught only an oblique view of a profile: a grizzled cheek, a longish sideburn, a ropey muscle in the neck. Another man followed, and the pair threaded their way along the aisle. The first man entered the bathroom in the plane's mid-section while his companion sat down in a nearby vacant seat.

That was funny, John thought, as though one of the

3 —

men were afraid to go to the bathroom alone and had to have his friend along just in case. He gave a smile at the thought, then buried his nose in the magazine.

The man locked the bathroom door and stood for a moment in front of the tiny sink and inset mirror. Yesterday had been his thirty-eighth birthday. He grimaced as though in pain. He wouldn't stand a chance at the trial, there were at least two bank clerks who could identify him. And with his record the judge would hit him with ten to twenty for sure. Which meant Will Bennett's life would be practically over when he got out. And all because of a burned-out headlight he didn't even know he had. When he saw the flashing red light and heard the siren, like a dope he had tried to outrun the police cruiser. And gotten himself caught when all that hick cop wanted was to caution him about the dead headlight. And he had been within fifty miles of the Canadian border too.

He looked in the wastepaper basket, searching for something to use as a weapon. Even an old razor blade would do. A couple of crumpled wash-and-dry napkins bearing the name, "Down-East Airways," a Hershey bar wrapper, half a dozen paper towels. His glance circled the tiny room. He read the sign above the toilet bowl: "Please don't throw waste paper materials or other foreign objects into the bowl." In a sudden fury he emptied the wastepaper basket into the toilet bowl and tried to flush it. The paper jammed and the bowl began to overflow. He grunted in satisfaction, then caught another glimpse of himself in the mirror. What he wouldn't give for a knife right now: he'd grab the stewardess and hijack the plane to Cuba. That mirror!

He swiftly got out of his jacket, then removed one shoe. Holding his jacket up against the mirror to muffle the noise, he swung the shoe so that the heel hit flat against the glass. The blow seemed to make no impact and he lifted away the jacket, expecting to see the mirror intact.

But a starburst of cracks radiated out from the center of the glass. Now if he could only get one of those pieces out, it would make a good dagger, good enough for what he had in mind.

He forced his thumbnail under the tip of a triangular-shaped piece and pulled outwards. The piece held fast, its edge caught under a lip of the stainless steel frame. He began to rock the point up and down, trying to flare the metal rim outwards. The plane hit another air pocket and a spurt of blood shot from the ball of his thumb. Instinctively he sucked at the cut, then lowered his hand to look at the wound. It was minor and would soon stop bleeding. He noted the raised red weal marks on his wrist. He had been cuffed all day in that damn lock-up, but thank God they had taken the cuffs off when he said he had to use the bathroom. After all, where could he run to?

He went back to work on the mirror and this time a long ten-inch piece of glass pulled out of the frame. He wrapped his hand around the wide part of the broken sliver and grunted with satisfaction. The rest of his makeshift dagger tapered to a very effective point.

He quickly put on his shoe, windmilled into the jacket, and picked up his dagger. Holding it inside his jacket, he opened the door with his left hand.

His escort stood up.

"Got a terrible gut-ache," he said to Detective Talmage, as though explaining the hand inside his jacket.

Detective Talmage nodded, then indicated that his prisoner should go ahead of him back down the aisle.

Still clutching the piece of glass, Bennett stepped out, moving toward the tiny serving alcove opposite the bathroom. Where the hell was the stewardess? He looked toward the rear of the plane and noted a stroke of luck. The other escort cop had his head down on his chest and was evidently taking a nap. He would have to make his move soon or lose his chance. He heard the sibilant whisper of metal rings sliding on a pole. The stewardess had just come through the curtain that separated first class from tourist. She let the curtain fall back and advanced on them with a smile. Then she stopped.

He had to get closer and away from his escort. "Here, miss," he said, holding out his hand with the piece of mirror in it, and backing into the dining alcove. "I found this on the bathroom floor."

As she stepped forward to take the object from him, he caught her outstretched hand, yanked her toward him, and spun her around so that she was facing the startled detective. Forcing her head high with his arm, he pressed the point of the spear-like piece of mirror against her throat with his other hand.

"Back up!" he snarled over her shoulder to the detective, who had moved into the alcove with them. "Back up or she gets it!"

Detective Talmage slowly backed up. In lockstep Bennett and his hostage followed. They came to the curtain.

"On through, and no tricks!"

They all went through the curtain and into the first-class section. And here Bennett realized a second stroke of luck. First class was empty of passengers.

"Hold it!" he said.

"Look Bennett," Talmage said quietly, "watch that glass. You've already cut her."

A thin trickle of blood ran down the neck of the stewardess, where the tip of the piece of mirror had pricked her skin.

"She'll be pouring blood if you don't do what I tell you," Bennett threatened.

The detective nodded. He had the message.

"Take that Police Special out of your shoulder holster and hold it by the barrel."

The detective did as he was told.

"Now, very slow, place the gun on that empty seat beside you there. And be careful, one wrong move and she gets it."

Again the detective did as he was told.

"Now, back up!"

Detective Talmage stepped back three paces. Forcing

the stewardess ahead, Bennett moved forward until he had reached the seat. Then in one fast motion, he dropped the piece of mirror, shoved the girl forward, and snatched up the gun. "Okay, both of you, make your way to the cockpit. And remember, I'm right behind you."

"We can't enter the flight deck," the stewardess said. "The door is locked while the plane is in the air." Despite her effort at control, her voice shook with fear. And although she had a key to the cockpit, she wasn't ready to let him know that yet.

"How do you talk to the pilot?" Bennett asked.

"Intercom phone." She pointed to one of the several phones that linked the flight deck with the rest of the cabin.

"Okay, call him and tell him I got a loaded gun pointed at the back of your head. If he doesn't want a dead stewardess on his hands, he'll open that door."

The stewardess lifted down the phone and talked softly into it for a minute or so. She tried very hard to control her shaking voice. She finished the conversation and the phone clattered as she put it back in its cradle and said, "The captain said to let you in. This way." She reached under her flight jacket for the key to the flight deck door. Beside her marched the detective, with Bennett bringing up the rear.

At the back of the plane, John stretched, gave a comfortable yawn, then said to Mark, "Funny way to run an airline. I just saw the stewardess kissing one of the passengers."

Mark laughed. "Wishful thinking. You hope our turn will come next."

"Never happen." John had earlier noticed the two men and the stewardess moving out of the alcove and through the curtain that led to first class. One of them must be sick, he thought, which is why the other guy was along. And now the stewardess was probably getting something for the sick passenger, aspirins or maybe some kind of airsick pills. Well, so far he himself felt fine, even though it was only his second time up in an airplane. Those bumps hadn't bothered him one bit. He glanced over at Mark, who was staring out the porthole window, then turned his attention to the magazine on his lap.

As yet no one in the back of the plane was aware that a hijacking was in progress. And in the cockpit, the hijacker barked out the one word that airline pilots all over the country had learned to dread.

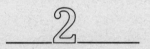

"Cuba?" The captain shot a quick look over at the co-pilot. The latter shrugged.

"Yeah, you heard me, Cuba! Havana, Cuba, and no stalling."

The flight deck was crowded. In addition to pilot and co-pilot, the detective and stewardess were jammed into the tiny area. Will Bennett, standing in the doorway, had his gun pointed at the captain. Now and again he would throw a quick glance behind, still worried about the other policeman in the back of the plane.

The captain ran his eye over the score of gauges on the instrument panels, then shook his head. "I don't have enough fuel for Cuba. I don't have an airport chart for Havana, and anyway I'm not qualified to fly an international run."

"Quit stalling and head this crate for Cuba." Bennett waved the gun menacingly.

"I tell you there's not enough fuel," the captain repeated. "It's almost two thousand miles to Cuba. Look, you see those needles?" The captain pointed to his fuel gauges. "They show that my tanks are less than half full. That gives us between seven and eight hundred miles, not even that if we run into any head winds."

"Then we gotta land somewhere for gas," Bennett said. "How far is it to Montreal?"

"Two-fifty, maybe three hundred miles."

"If we come down in Montreal, and fill her up and let the passengers go, could you make it to Havana in one hop?"

"Yeah, but look, why don't I set her down at Logan in Boston, or Kennedy in New York? They're both on the way."

"And have the F.B.I. waiting? Forget it. I'm not wanted in Canada, they won't be so anxious to get hold of me. Turn her around and put her down in Montreal."

The captain put the plane into a slow bank. "Now look," he said, "I'll have to call the airport and let them know we're coming in. There's information I need to make a landing, descent plans, and I'll want them to head off any incoming flights when we arrive."

"Okay, but no tricks. I'm good for twenty years if I'm caught. I'll die first and I don't give a darn if I take the whole plane along."

"Relax," the pilot said. "You let us release the passengers in Montreal and that's all I'm concerned about. After that we fly you straight to Havana.''

Bennett nodded.

''Frequency thirty-one hundred,'' the captain called. The co-pilot tuned the radio to the 3100 frequency. Although Bennett did not know it, ground stations were now aware that a skyjacking was in progress. The 3100 frequency was used by pilots only in the event of a skyjacking, and ground stations, including the controllers at various airports, would now refrain from calling the captain until they heard from him. This was to allow the captain to take complete control of the situation in regard to his plane, if necessary to cut off all communication from the ground if such calls were causing the hijacker to panic.

Will Bennett pointed the gun at the stewardess. ''Okay, you go back to my seat and tell the other cop there to give you his gun. Tell him any tricks, any sign of him putting his nose into the cockpit, and his buddy here gets one between the eyes. You got that?''

''Yes. What shall I tell the passengers? They may suspect something.''

''Just stall them, tell them everything's fine. No one will get hurt if they just keep to their seats and mind their own business.''

The stewardess left the cockpit, closing the door behind her. Bennett came all the way into the flight deck and waggled the gun at Detective Talmage. ''You, sit over there behind the pilot.''

Talmage went over and sat down in the observer's

seat behind the captain. Bennett took up position behind the co-pilot, his heavy revolver now pointed at the captain. From this position he could watch all three men and still keep an eye on the door.

The captain spoke into the mike. "Down-East Airways Flight 147 calling control tower in Montreal. Come in Montreal."

There was a burst of radio crackle, then a voice came through. "Down-East Flight 147, this is Montreal Airport. Go ahead."

"DEA 147 Lewisburg to Boston flight. We have a problem on board. Request emergency clearance to land."

"DEA 147, this is Montreal. You are cleared, immediate, on runway seven."

"Yes, affirmative on runway seven."

"Ceiling Montreal nine hundred, visibility two miles, wind six knots. Do you have a chart for Montreal?"

"Affirmative on plate for Montreal," the captain responded.

"DEA 147, do you need emergency equipment?"

"Negative on emergency equipment. Repeat, negative."

Although the controller at Montreal Airport already knew, thanks to the 3100 frequency, that a hijacking was in progress, he could not know what violence might have already broken out, or whether the pilot was in need of an ambulance, police, or fire-fighting equipment.

Bennett listened attentively, alert for any trickery.

13 —

Gun pointed at the pilot, he stood sideways behind the co-pilot, his gaze moving back and forth between the captain, the detective, and the door that opened on the passageway between the flight deck and the captain.

"Cruising altitude, nine thousand feet. E.T.A. twenty-two minutes."

"You are clear at nine thousand," Montreal responded.

"What is your ground elevation?" the captain asked.

The intercom phone buzzed and the co-pilot spoke into it. "Yes, all right, okay." He turned to Bennett. "It's the stewardess."

"Does she have the gun?"

"Yes."

"Okay, tell her to open the door nice and slow and tell her that if anyone else except her comes in, I blow your brains out." Bennett pressed the muzzle of his gun against the back of the co-pilot's head as he relayed the message.

The door opened slowly and the stewardess stood there, visibly pale beneath her makeup, the gun held in her right hand, resting on her out-thrust palm.

Bennett nodded. "Good."

In the observer's seat behind the captain, Detective Talmage was poised and ready, his right hand inches above the curved handle of the captain's dispatch case, which the captain had earlier placed on the floor behind his seat. The detective had been thinking ahead and knew that when the stewardess came forward to hand over the gun, Bennett's view of him would be temporarily blocked. If a diversion were created, it should be possible to grab the other gun and turn the tables on the hijacker.

The stewardess took two steps forward and extended her arm. At that moment Detective Talmage leaped up and swung the briefcase. It narrowly missed the stewardess and sailed across the cabin to catch Bennett on the forehead. He grunted and staggered back a step. At almost the same instant the detective snatched the gun out of the stewardess's hand.

"No, no . . ." she screamed.

Talmage took quick aim at Bennett and pulled the trigger. There was a click and the detective swore.

Bennett, recovered now, fired three times, three deafening explosions. The stewardess spun backward, the detective grabbed at his stomach with both hands, and the pilot slapped at his neck. Then Talmage sank back onto the observer's seat, still holding his stomach, and slowly pitched to the floor. The pilot glanced down at the fallen detective, then reached forward to the controls and automatically made a correction, trimming his plane. He started to say something but found that he could not speak.

Coming out of the shock of the explosions, the co-pilot turned around and saw that the detective and stewardess were shot and lying on the cockpit floor. He looked over at the captain, at the blood that was bubbling out of the side of the captain's neck and running down his white shirt. The co-pilot's immediate thought was that the hijacker intended to kill everyone in the cockpit, that he was bent on suicide, on bringing the plane and passengers down with him. He therefore swung his arm, hitting Bennett on the side of the head. Then he jumped from his seat and grappled with him, trying to wrest the gun out of his hands. Bennett fired three more times and the co-pilot, though mortally wounded, succeeded in twisting the gun out of the other man's grip. The co-pilot's last conscious thought was one of satisfaction. He had foiled the skyjacking. Someone was taking the gun. Good . . . things were under control now and the passengers were safe. Suddenly he slid to the floor.

Will Bennett looked around, actually shocked at the scene in the cabin. Three were either dead or dying and the pilot was wounded. He had not meant to really kill anyone, each time he had reacted in panic.

He reached down and took the gun from the co-pilot's now lifeless fingers. Not sure exactly how many times he had fired the weapon, he swung the chamber out and checked the six cylindrical compartments. They were empty. Still he had the other gun. He stooped to pick it up and remembered the detective's attempt to shoot. He checked the chamber on the second gun. It too was empty, the cop at the back of the plane having taken the precaution to remove all the bullets from the weapon before handing it to the stewardess. The hijacker was now unarmed and at the mercy of anyone who entered the flight deck.

He looked across at the captain, who sat there quietly flying the machine as though it were a perfectly normal flight. Blood still oozed from the wound on his neck.

"Hey! Can you put this thing down at Montreal?" Bennett shouted. He waved his useless gun at the pilot.

The pilot nodded. He picked up the logbook, opened it on his lap, and switched on a tiny spotlight in the cabin ceiling. Taking a pencil out of his pocket, he wrote on a blank page of the logbook, "Can fly okay but can't speak." He held the logbook in one hand and Bennett came over to read the message.

"Okay, you fly it and get us down at Montreal."

The pilot scribbled another message on the page and again held it up.

"I need someone, talk to Montreal," Bennett read aloud. For a moment he was puzzled. Then he understood and said, "Okay, you write down what you want me to say."

The pilot nodded and mouthed the word, "later."

Bennett went back and sat in the co-pilot's seat, to stare vacantly through the windshield at the darkening sky outside.

And the plane droned on through the cold March sky, at 9,000 feet altitude, with a dying pilot at the controls and all radio contact with ground stations now broken off. Controllers would not call the aircraft unless the pilot contacted them first, and the doomed pilot could not use his voice.

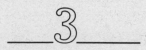

3

Will Bennett tried to peer through the windshield. He could see little, except ragged wisps and
scarves of fog that went streaming past through the late
afternoon light. He looked over at the pilot. "You still
okay?"

The pilot nodded. The pilot was far from being all
right. He had to constantly dab at his mouth with a
handkerchief to soak up the blood that seeped out
through his lips. He felt weak and was afraid of passing
out but there was nothing he could do about it. There
was no one else to fly the plane. So he concentrated on
the correct bearing and altitude and tried to keep his
craft reasonably level. With any kind of luck he would
set them all down in one piece at Montreal Airport.
After that someone else could take over and straighten
everything out.

In the back of the cabin Marshal James O'Connor sat paralyzed with indecision. He had heard the series of shots and knew them for what they were. But he had no idea what was going on. If the prisoner had been overpowered, then Talmage would have come back to let him know, or at least sent the stewardess back to tell him. But so far no one had appeared. Perhaps Bennett had only fired a few warning shots? But so many of them? There had been at least six reports.

Marshal O'Connor sat on the edge of his seat and stared up the aisle. He might leave his seat and go as far as the first class section. He dare not go any further, especially after that warning from Bennett that Talmage would get it if anyone tried to enter the cockpit. But perhaps he might contact the stewardess and find out what was going on. Something had obviously happened.

No one else in the back of the plane seemed to pay any attention to the shots. Most of the passengers were either asleep or trying to sleep, and the series of noises from inside the closed, almost soundproofed cockpit had sounded no worse than a stewardess slamming some pots or steel trays around. Which is exactly what John Jenkins thought the sounds were when he first heard them. After all, the stewardess had warned them, a few minutes ago, that they might run into some turbulence but that everything was just fine. Of course they hadn't seen the stewardess since but she was probably catching up on her work, or was up front talking to one of the crew. Someone was going up the aisle now, probably looking for her. John was going to comment on her absence to his seat companion, but when he turned his head Mark smiled and said, "My ears are popping, I guess we're coming down."

"We can't be at Boston yet," John said. He leaned across Mark to look out the porthole. There was nothing to be seen except shredded curtains of fog, with patches of steel-gray sky showing through here and there. But then, for just a moment, he thought he saw a mountain-top. "Hey, trees!"

John drew back to let Mark share the view and out of the corner of his eye caught sight of someone hurrying toward them down the aisle.

"Yeah, I think I see mountains," Mark said.

John crowded back to the window and both boys tried to see through the murk outside. But the fog was im-penetrable and after a moment or two they lost interest.

John stretched out in his seat and put his head back on the headrest. Beside him, Mark frowned and said, "Hey, you know something? I got a funny feeling that . . ."

But Mark never got a chance to finish his sentence because at that moment the plane gave a gut-wrenching buck, as though it had just slammed an invisible trip wire. A briefcase went flying through the air and hit John on the side of the head. The blow stunned him and he slumped forward in his seat, only to be whipped back again as the plane surged forward, accompanied by the sound of snapping trees and tortured metal, reports that rang out with the startling immediacy of rifle shots.

A huge hand jammed John's head down into his lap.

— 20

For a moment he could not see, then realized that a coat was covering him. Panicky, he snatched at it, afraid of smothering. And still the plane moved, grinding forward, snapping trees and leaving bigger and bigger chunks of metal in its wake. Dimly John was aware of screams, loud ripping noises, someone moaning, a harsh smoky smell. He lowered his hands from his face. The point of an umbrella protruded from the back of the seat in front of him. On impact, the umbrella had been hurled like a spear, driving right through the seat back.

An explosion rocked the plane. John felt his legs lifting into the air. One of his knees slammed into his mouth and he caught the salty taste of blood. Somewhere in front of him, a voice pleaded. ''Oh help, please somebody, I'm hurt bad. Oh help, oh help . . .''

A momentary silence fell and John looked up the incline of the aisle. Ahead of him the passageway ended in space. Although the air was full of smoke and fog, he could make out the tops of trees against a dark gray sky, an early evening sky. Suddenly he was aware of the cold March air.

''I think I'm alive,'' he said to himself in wonder.

''Let's get out of here before she goes on fire,'' someone shouted.

John fumbled at his seat belt, trying to unbuckle it. The whole belt came away in his hands. It had torn loose from its seat anchors. To his surprise he found that he could stand up, though the sharp upward tilt of the plane fuselage made it difficult to keep his balance.

A hand caught his arm. "You okay?" A bloody face that he did not recognize loomed over him.

"I think so."

"Then give me a hand," Mark said. "There's an old man back here somewhere."

John followed Mark as the two boys made their way down the aisle.

"Fire!" someone screamed. John turned around. The night sky outside the fuselage had turned brilliant orange as sheets of flame lit up the sky.

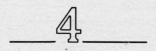

4

The plane had flown into the saddle of a mountain and broken in two. The front two-thirds of the aircraft, comprising the flight deck, first class, and about half of the tourist section, skidded some fifty yards further than the tail section, skidded just far enough to topple over the edge of a steep cliff that formed one boundary of the saddle. The front section burst into flames as a result of this secondary impact and there was no question of anyone inside surviving the double crash and resulting fire. By some miracle the seven people sitting in the back three or four rows of seats in the tail section came through the ordeal alive, though all had cuts and bruises of one sort or another, and one man was unconscious.

John had meant to sit down somewhere and calmly

try to figure out a way to stop the bleeding in his mouth, but instead he found himself helping Mark drag a man out of the plane's torn fuselage. Stumbling in the dark, his hands under the man's legs, John said, "Where will we put him?"

"Anywhere."

"Is he dead?"

"Probably."

They laid the man down on a clear patch of ground and John straightened up. He was still dazed. He looked blankly at Mark for a moment and then asked, his voice breaking, "What do we do with that thing sticking out of him?"

"What thing?"

"That tube." A thin, round piece of aluminum stuck out of the man's chest.

"God, I'm not a doctor!" Mark snapped. "How do I know what to do?"

John bent down and caught the piece of tubing. He gave a gentle tug and the tube came smoothly out. The man's shirt around the hole was sopping with blood but it was too dark to see how bad the wound was.

John straightened up. An orange glow lit up the sky somewhere ahead of him and his nostrils were assailed by the harsh acrid smell of burning gasoline.

A girl stumbled past in the semi-darkness and John recognized Annie Hopson.

"My parents are supposed to meet me!" she cried. "Where are they?"

John caught her by the arm. "Are you all right?"

"Where are my parents? They were supposed to be here," she said, trying to pull free.

"Take it easy now." John turned his head away and spat out a mouthful of blood. He drew a quick gulp of air, then said, "Let's find somewhere to sit down." He led Annie away from the tail section.

He found Desmond and the old man sitting on some cushions taken from the plane.

"Let her share that cushion with you," he said to Desmond.

Desmond moved over and Annie suddenly collapsed. For a minute her shoulders heaved with a harsh dry sobbing. Carefully the old man leaned over, draped a garment over her shoulders, then awkwardly patted her back. "There now, it's all over and you're safe." He looked up at John and said, "She's in shock."

"Yeah, I guess."

"By the way, thanks for helping me."

"Helping you?"

"Yes, you and that other young man helped me out of the plane. Don't you remember?"

"Yeah, sure." John turned away, confused. He didn't remember. Something was wrong. He had just helped Mark carry someone out of the plane but that man was dead or dying, the man with the wound in his chest. Had he helped carry someone else out of the plane? And where was Mark?

John stumbled through some bushes. He headed for

the tail section. He ought to find Mark, and he ought to see about that man. Maybe they could do something for him, make a bandage for that wound or something.

He stumbled over a root and threw out his hands to break the fall. As he hit the ground, a pain knifed through his jaw, bringing tears to his eyes. Ahead of him he saw a dim figure bending over the man that he and Mark had helped out of the wreckage. Was that Mark or someone else? He would call to him. For some reason he couldn't get up. And the pain in his jaw was killing him.

"Can someone help me?" he called weakly. Then he passed out.

When he came to he was dimly aware of being the object of discussion. "What's wrong with the black kid?" someone was asking.

Warily John opened his eyes. He was lying full length on the ground, his head on a seat cushion, a coat stretched over him.

"He's lost a lot of blood," Mark said. "He was bleeding from the mouth but it's stopped now."

John tried to sit up. He finally managed to push himself into a sitting position, using the trunk of a tree as a support. Across from him sat the old man and one of the middle-aged men who had been seated in the very back row of the tourist section. Behind them, stretched out on the ground, was the man he and Mark had pulled from the plane. Someone had lit a small fire.

"How are you feeling?" Desmond asked. He and

Annie sat on one side of the fire, and Mark sat across from them.

"A bit groggy," John said. "I lost some teeth." His tongue explored a cavity on one side of his jaw. At least one tooth was gone completely, while another had sheared off at gum level. He realized now that the intense pain in his jaw had come from that broken-off tooth and not a broken jaw as he had feared.

A moan came from the man stretched out on the ground and John was surprised. Somehow he had assumed the man was dead. He walked over to him and knelt down. The hair just above the man's forehead was matted with blood and more congealed blood could be seen on the bridge of his nose and clotted in his eyebrows. The wound in his chest was hidden by a blanket that someone had tucked around him.

Another wave of pain and nausea hit John and he closed his eyes, blacking out for a minute. When he came to the middle-aged man was talking.

". . . his name's Will Bennett and he's wanted for bank robbery. Me and my partner, Detective Talmage, were escorting him to Boston to turn him over to the F.B.I. Somehow he got hold of the stewardess and forced her and Talmage into the cockpit where he tried to hijack the plane. Something must have gone wrong, there were shots, and the next thing I knew we were crashing."

"Hijacked! I can't believe it," Annie exclaimed. "Remember what I told you, Desmond?"

"Don't remind me," Desmond groaned.

"You're a policeman, too, then?" Mark asked.

"Yes. Marshal Jim O'Connor of the Adams County Police."

"What's he saying?" Mark asked, pointing to the hijacker.

"Just moaning is all," Marshal O'Connor said. "That's a bad wound he's got there."

"Lawn mower's on the fritz," the hijacker mumbled.

"Aw shut up," the marshal said.

"We ought to let him die," Desmond said. "I mean he's a murderer, right?"

"We better start worrying about ourselves," John spoke up. "We may all die if we don't get out of here."

"I don't want to die," Annie said very calmly, very simply, as though she were saying, "I don't want to go for a walk."

"You okay now?" John asked her. "For a while there you were really out of it."

"Just my eyes." Annie reached up and tenderly touched her cheek. Something had hit her a sharp blow on the bridge of the nose and across the eyebrows. Already the flesh around both eyes was beginning to puff up.

Another moan came from the hijacker, then the words, "ten-four."

"What does that mean?" John asked.

"Nothing," the marshal said. "Just gibberish is all. He's probably got a concussion."

"Do we have anyone fit enough to go for firewood?"

— 28

the old man asked. "If we're going to stay here all night, we're going to need more firewood."

"I'm sorry, but my hip's so bad, I can hardly walk," Marshal O'Connor said.

"I'll go." Mark came over to John and laid a hand on his shoulder. "Can you help me?"

John nodded, then carefully got to his feet. He was afraid of feeling faint again, but the pain and nausea seemed to have passed for the moment.

The two boys turned away from the fire and began to forage for dry wood. They soon found the fallen skeleton of a medium-sized tree. They snapped off all the dead limbs, carried them over, and piled them up beside the fire. Then they dragged over the stripped trunk and centered it on the flames. When it had burned in two, both halves could be fed gradually into the fire. They managed to locate another, smaller dead trunk and dragged that one over too.

John sat down and spread his hands to the blaze. At least they had fire to ward off the cold. First thing in the morning, search planes should be out looking for the wreckage.

"Do you think anyone knows where we are?" Desmond asked.

"Don't worry, they'll be out looking for us," the old man said.

"If the weather isn't too bad," O'Connor added.

"Are the people who were in the front of the plane all . . ." Annie began.

"Yes," Mark answered quickly. "I looked down the

cliff at that fire. There's no way they could have survived it and the crash."

"So there's just the seven of us then?" John said. If I were home now, he thought to himself, I'd play a number ending in seven.

John leaned back against the tree, closed his eyes, and tried to go to sleep. All that kept popping into his mind were images of Sal's Candy Store on 122nd Street and the guys who hung out there—Big Chooch, Caddy, Stitch, Geronimo, Father-of-our-Country, whose real name was George Lincoln Washington. If the guys could see me now, they'd bust a gut laughing, John thought. He heard the old man's voice rambling on and opened his eyes.

"A day younger than the century," the old man's voice quavered. "Born January second, nineteen hundred . . . retired from the Army some twenty years ago . . . name is Lusty . . . Edward Everett Lusty . . ."

"Are you all right, sir?" Desmond asked, touching him on the shoulder.

"Yes, yes, a bit dazed is all. Just checking myself out," the old man smiled. "I was dozing when the plane crashed, and for a few minutes there I thought I was back in the Battle of the Bulge. Then these two boys helped me out. How about you?"

Desmond rubbed his side and winced. "I dunno . . . feels like I cracked a rib or something. Every time I draw a deep breath, I get this sharp pain . . ." Desmond stopped—it hurt too much to talk.

John thought of his own wound then. He gathered some saliva and spat it into his cupped palm. It seemed clear, with no color of blood. He wiped his hand on his trousers and looked across at Mark. "How about you?" he asked.

Mark patted the top of his head. His forehead was still covered with a crust of dried blood. "I got a bad gash up here but it's not bleeding any more. Also something hit my thigh, which is sore as hell. Otherwise I'm okay."

The hijacker began to moan again. Blood bubbles foamed between his lips, then burst as he tried to talk.

"What's he saying?" Annie asked.

" 'Listen' or 'Lisabeth' or 'Liz,' I think," the old man said.

Something cool touched John on the forehead. "It's snowing," he said, half to himself.

"Oh man, that's all we need," Desmond protested.

"Liz? Liz?" the hijacker called clearly, then lapsed into silence.

"I'm cold," Annie said.

When the first gray light filtered through the trees, John woke up. He had not really slept but had shifted back and forth between daydreams and being aware that he was a survivor of a plane crash somewhere in a forest. Now and again he vaguely sensed movement, someone feeding the fire from time to time. Now two things were immediately apparent to him: during the early hours a very light dusting of snow had fallen, and someone had pulled the blanket up over the hijacker's face. John looked across at Annie and Desmond, who were huddled under a pile of coats. Mark was also motionless, his head down on his drawn-up knees and a coat draped over his shoulders. Only the marshal and Mr. Lusty were awake.

"Is he dead?" John asked.

"I'm afraid so," Mr. Lusty said.

"Bought it, and a good thing," Marshal O'Connor said.

"Poor guy." John spoke almost to himself. Somehow the deaths of the other passengers didn't seem real but this was different. There he was right in front of them, stretched out on the ground, a body, stiff with death.

"Listen!" O'Connor said. "Think of the dead people down over the mountain. He deserves everything he got. He had it coming to him."

The marshal's angry words woke the others. Mark stirred himself and stood up. Swinging his arms under his armpits to warm up, he said, each word accompanied by a little puff of vapor, "What do we do with him now?"

"We're not gonna worry about that," the marshal said. "First thing is for a couple of you kids to scout around and see if you can spot anything."

John glanced at Mark. It looked like they were elected again.

"You know what to look for?" the marshal said.

"Any signs of civilization," John replied.

"Also look for a stream or a snowbank," Mr. Lusty said. "We're going to need water."

John stood up. He felt his tender jaw.

"You okay?" Mark asked.

The broken-off tooth still pained him when his tongue accidentally jarred it, and his whole jawbone was sore. But otherwise he was sound. "I'm okay," he nodded.

"Good luck," Desmond called as they left the clearing.

Mark and John worked their way around the wreckage, then followed the wide swath of fallen trees that the front half of the plane had leveled. They soon came to the edge of the cliff. The precipice was not quite as steep as it had looked in the dark last night, with the fire blazing hundreds of feet below. The face of the cliff was a gray clay, scarred with gullies. There were half a dozen deep gouges across the slope, where the rolling plane had torn out chunks of fresh earth. Here and there bits of twisted aluminum lay on the slope. Several hundred feet below them, the remains of the plane had caught in a clump of jack pine on a fifty-foot-wide ledge. The trees were burned of all their branches, a dozen nude blackened trunks rising above the gutted hulk of the fuselage. Another hundred feet below this pile of twisted metal, one of the engines rested against the trunk of a large evergreen. Although a wisp of smoke still rose from the wreckage, and the air still smelled of burning cloth and scorched metal, the snow had already started to erase the evidence.

Mark shook his head. "Even if someone were still alive down there, there's just no way we could reach them."

"Wouldn't do any good even if we did get down there," John sighed. "Nobody could have lived through that."

Together the two boys scanned the surrounding terrain. Half a dozen tree-covered mountains rose in succeeding heights to the horizon line. They carefully examined all the visible ground, the valleys and the draws, the sides of the mountains. There was no evidence anywhere of human habitation; no houses, no roads, no electric or telephone lines.

"Wild country," Mark said.

"Yeah. Look how low those clouds are. No planes are going to find us today."

"I guess not," Mark agreed.

"Let's go back and follow around the side of that hill."

The two boys struck out through the trees and soon came across a faint trail.

"Hey, this must lead somewhere," John said.

They came to an open hillside but the path petered out, or rather turned into a dozen fainter deer trails. Halfway across the hillside, they stopped for a moment to survey their surroundings.

"Hey, I see a house, I think," Mark said and pointed.

In the bottom of a draw, sitting on a patch of flat cleared land, was a small cabin.

"Hey man, I sure hope somebody's at home," John said.

The boys cut downhill, worked their way through a belt of trees on a ridge top, then dropped down another hillside and crossed the flat ground toward the cabin.

As they approached, John said, "Look, there's a creek. On the other side, over there!"

"Great!" Mark said. "But the cabin looks empty."

No smoke rose from the chimney. The small woodpile, stacked between the trunks of two fir trees, was gray with age, the wood having been cut long years before. The window on one side of the cabin was overgrown with vines, Virginia creeper that stretched all the way up and onto the wood shake roof.

John stepped up on the small porch in front of the door. There was a loud crash as he went through the floorboards. "Shoot! Everything's rotten." He lifted his feet from the broken boards, then swung the door back on its hinges and stepped over the threshold. Mark came in and for a moment both boys examined the dim interior. There was a rough stone fireplace, and along one wall a low platform, obviously meant for a bed. On top of the platform was the remains of a mattress that mice and chipmunks had riddled for nesting materials. A rough wooden table sat against the other wall, two cut log rounds serving as chairs. On one wall beside the fireplace hung a small wooden cabinet, its door askew.

Mark walked over to the cabinet and tried to open the door. The remaining hinge let go and the door fell to the floor. Inside, the shelves were bare, except for a scattering of shredded pine cones, left behind by a chipmunk.

"Well, it isn't much," Mark said.

"Better than staying out in the open."

"That's for sure," Mark agreed. He went back to the door and looked out. Long before the cabin had been built here, he thought, the place had probably been used as an Indian camp. It was a natural, water nearby, lots of shelter, lots of cover for game and wild animals.

"Hey, tell you what," John called. "Why don't you go back for the others? I'll stay here and get the cabin ready."

Mark shook his head. "I think we should both go back. Suppose some of them want to stay near the plane?"

"Come on, man, you're not making sense," John argued. "We got shelter and water here for everyone."

"We two should stick together."

"Why? You can find your way back alone, can't you?"

"Yes, but just in case. You never can tell what might happen. It's just not a good idea to split up."

"Okay, okay," John said. "We both go back then."

"Anyway some of them will need help getting here," Mark said.

John let his irritation show. "I said okay, didn't I?"

Mark went outside and waited for John to follow him. Then he turned and said, "Let's take a look at that stream on the other side of the clearing before we head back."

They walked across the open patch of land and stopped at the edge of a narrow creek.

"I wouldn't exactly call that a river," John said.

"No, but we can get drinking water from it."

It was the sort of creek that would dry up completely in late summer, a long series of shallow pools connected by a trickle of water. Mark knelt down over one of the pools, cupped his hands, and lifted water to his mouth. He scooped up four or five handfuls, then exclaimed, "Wow, that's cold!" He dried his hands on his jacket and waited until John had taken a drink.

Then both boys headed back to the plane.

5

When Mark and John returned to the others, they found that Annie and Desmond and Marshal O'Connor had somehow managed to drag the body of the dead hijacker over to the tail end of the fuselage, covering it with pieces of aluminum taken from the wreckage. Heavy stones had been placed on top to keep wild animals from molesting the rude burial spot.

"I think we ought to move to the cabin," Mark advised the others, after telling them of their discovery.

After some discussion it was agreed that the shift would be made in stages. Mark and John would help O'Connor and Mr. Lusty to the cabin, while Desmond and Annie would look around in the wreckage for food and whatever other articles might come in handy. When the marshal and Mr. Lusty were settled, Mark and John would return for Annie and Desmond and lead them back to the cabin and help carry whatever salvageable articles had turned up.

Annie watched the two young men leave with the marshal and Mr. Lusty. O'Connor was limping badly and Lusty was being helped along by Mark. She turned to Desmond. "How is your side?"

Desmond placed a hand on his ribs. "They still hurt but I think it's just a bruise, not broken. If I straighten up suddenly, or take a deep breath, though, I really feel it."

Annie nodded, then felt the flesh around her cheekbones. She had two black eyes, the skin swollen up and discolored so badly that the top half of her nose appeared to be missing.

"Can you see all right?" Desmond asked.

"Sort of." Annie peered out of the two slits beneath her brows. Her bloodshot eyes could still see anything directly in front of her, but she had lost most of her peripheral vision due to the swollen flesh at each corner of her eyes.

"Why don't you stay here at the fire," Desmond said, "while I scout around?"

He went over and climbed up into the wreck, then began to drop blankets, pillows, and coats down to Annie. Soon a pile of clothing lay on the ground. He continued to drop small suitcases, briefcases, and flight bags taken from the overhead storage racks. One of the flight bags belonged to Annie herself and as soon as she caught it, she placed it on the ground and pulled back the zipper. "Hey, wow!" she cried out. "Let's see what we have in here."

She pulled out a couple of paperback books, a sheaf of pamphlets about Livingstone College, and a yellow apple. She held up the fruit. "Hey, Desmond, we have an apple. I forgot all about it."

Desmond came to the mouth of the fuselage. "Big deal," he called down. "One apple for six people."

"Well, it's better than nothing."

She squatted over another briefcase and opened it. It was jammed full of files. She rummaged through some documents, then announced, "Nothing, just a bunch of papers."

"Here catch!" Desmond held a large stainless steel bowl in both hands. He let it drop to the ground and Annie retrieved it.

"We can use that to hold water." Desmond turned and went back into the fuselage. Soon he was tugging on a piece of black cable. For a moment he forgot all about his ribs and pulled too hard, only to double up with a sudden knife-like thrust of pain in his side. He waited for the pain to go away, then went back to the cable. Finally he pulled it free and found that it contained half a dozen different colored electric wires that apparently ran from the flight deck back to the tail. When he got the strands all separated, he had a coil of fine copper wire over fifty feet long. He dropped the coil to Annie. "Can't tell when this might come in useful." Minutes later he was dropping a long tube of several dozen wax paper cups. It took him an hour to clean out the fuselage and when he had finished, he dropped down from the plane and joined Annie at the pile of clothing and salvaged articles.

"One lousy apple is all," Desmond said. "Did you search through the pockets of those coats?"

"Most of them."

"Well, let's go through them all, maybe we'll find a candy bar or something."

They turned up nothing new, except two rolls of camera film and a deck of cards.

They replenished the fire, then sat for a moment to warm their hands. Desmond kicked at a burning branch. "Do you think if I scout out from the plane you'll be all right on your own?"

"Oh, sure. What is there to be afraid of?" Annie said.

"What I'll do is, I'll shout every once in a while in case you need me for anything."

"Okay."

After a short rest, Desmond stood up and moved off through the trees in the direction from which the plane had come down. He found plenty of pieces of torn aluminum. Every once in a while he shouted, then waited for an answering shout from Annie. Finally he ran across a tan garment hung up in the low branches of an evergreen. He moved over to it and got it disentangled. It was a raincoat and he thrust a hand into one pocket and felt a bulky object. He pulled it out and found himself looking at two sandwiches wrapped in clear plastic wrap. One was cheese and ham. The other looked like egg salad.

He didn't think twice but quickly unwrapped the egg sandwich and crammed one half into his mouth. He put the other sandwich in his pocket. The egg and bread and mayonnaise tasted delicious. He briefly debated taking the other half sandwich back with him but he couldn't figure out a way to explain how he found only half an egg salad sandwich. To heck with it, he decided, and crammed the other half into his mouth.

He had just begun to chew on it when he heard Annie's call. For a moment he panicked and began to choke on the sandwich. Coughing and choking, he managed to get the ball of mush out of his mouth. It fell to the ground and he stared at it.

For the third time Annie's call sounded through the trees. He wiped the tears from his eyes and decided that he had better answer or she might come looking for him. He lifted his voice and, in a sort of rage, howled out his frustration, "All right, all right, I'm coming!"

He bent down and picked up the mushy blob of sandwich. He ignored the dirt that clung to the mixture and popped the doughy ball into his mouth and resumed chewing. When he was all through, he dropped to his knees, scratched a hole in the semi-frozen ground, and buried the plastic wrapping. Then, worried that traces of egg salad might still be visible on his mouth, he vigorously wiped his face on the lining of the raincoat, scrubbing so hard at his mouth and chin and teeth that it was almost painful, as though by scrubbing hard enough he could wipe away what he had done, could wipe that egg salad sandwich completely out of existence, out of his memory even.

Ten minutes later he was back at the fire.

"I was beginning to worry," Annie said.

Desmond pulled forth the sandwich and held it up. "I found one sandwich, ham and cheese," he said, then mentally kicked himself for saying "one." He should have said "a sandwich."

"Great!" she said, holding out a white box.

"What's in there?" Desmond asked.

"Two pounds of hard candy balls." She lifted the package and rattled it. "Hear that?"

"Not bad," Desmond said. "Must be fifty candies in there. How long do you think that'll keep us alive?"

"Well, certainly, not forever, but a sandwich, an apple, and a box of candies is a lot better than nothing."

"I suppose," Desmond agreed. "At least we have plenty of warm clothing. We're going to need it, too. I practically froze last night."

"Me, too."

They sat down in front of the fire to wait for the return of Mark and John. It seemed like hours but finally they heard voices and then saw the welcome sight of the two boys coming toward them through the trees.

The two young men dropped to their haunches in front of the fire.

"Did you find any food?" Mark asked.

Annie showed them the apple, sandwich, and box of candies.

"Great!" John said, hungrily.

"First thing we got to do," Mark said, "is leave a sign in the wreckage." He rummaged around and finally tore the backing out of a briefcase. With a felt tip pen that he found in another attaché case, he inked in directions for any rescue party that might reach the scene. "There are six survivors in a cabin two miles west of here. Look for smoke!"

"Give it to me," John said. "I'll put it inside the fuselage somewhere." He took the sign and climbed up into the wreck. He managed to prop the cardboard into a porthole window where it was secure from the elements. Then he rejoined the others around the fire.

"I'm telling you," Mark was saying, "that old man Lusty is really something. He's got more nerve than any of us."

"What's the cabin like?" Desmond asked.

"It's shelter. We finally managed to get a fire going. At first we were smoked out. There was an old crow's nest blocking the chimney, but John climbed up on the roof and cleared the chimney with a long stick."

"Anyone need a pair of gloves?" Annie asked. "We found two pair, one wool and the other leather."

John took the woolen gloves and tried them on. They could have been made for him.

"Well, we better start back," Mark said, getting to his feet.

They managed to bundle up everything except some

extra pillows which they placed inside the fuselage in case they might want to come back for them. Then, bundles resting on their shoulders, they headed for the cabin.

Marshal O'Connor and Mr. Lusty met them at the door of the cabin. As the marshal held out his arms to take some of the load, John noticed red welts around both his wrists. He shrugged it off—everyone had welts and bruises of one sort or another.

"Food?" O'Connor asked.

"One sandwich, one apple, and a box of hard candies," Desmond said, moving the objects carefully to one side.

"How should we split it up?" John asked.

"Before we split up the food, we should decide on some other things," Mr. Lusty said.

"Like what?" O'Connor asked.

"Someone should hike out and try to get help," Lusty said.

"I think we should all stay near the wreckage in case search planes are out looking for us," the marshal countered.

"If we had plenty of food," Lusty said. "Then I would agree and count on someone finding us in the next week or two. But there isn't much, and without food . . ."

"Where do you think we are?" Annie interrupted.

"Somewhere in Maine is my guess," Mr. Lusty said.

"I know the plane changed direction about five minutes before we came down," Mark said.

"If someone does go for help, how will they know which way to go?" John asked.

"You just follow the creek out there downstream," Mr. Lusty said. "Sooner or later it will lead you to a house or a farm or some sort of civilization."

John looked over at Mark for a long moment. It looked like they, or at least he, had already been picked. He was about to say something to that effect when Annie picked up the stainless steel bowl and announced, "I'm going for water."

"I'll get more firewood," Mark said.

As soon as Mark and Annie came back, everyone crowded up to the fire and sat down on the floor.

"At least we're in out of the cold and the wet, in front of a nice warm fire," Annie said.

"And even if we haven't got much food, we've got each other and plenty of water," Desmond added.

"How long do you think we can go without food?" Mark asked.

"That depends on health, age, and physical activity," Mr. Lusty said. "Some of you young people could last six weeks, maybe even a week or two longer."

"And how long do you think it might be before we're rescued?" John asked.

Mr. Lusty shook his head. "There's no telling. It's still only mid-March. An inch or two of snow and the crash site will be covered. At this altitude it could be six weeks before the snow melted."

The arithmetic was obvious to everyone.

"Somebody *has* to hike out," John said, looking at Mark.

"Today?" Mark asked.

"Why not?" John countered. "The sooner we get started, Mark, the better. It's still only mid-day."

Mark shrugged. "Let's think about it for a while. What's the hurry?"

A silence fell over the group as each one contemplated his plight. Finally Annie spoke up. "You know, there's something that keeps bothering me about all this."

"You mean you don't like what's happening?" John laughed sarcastically.

"All right, all right," Annie said. "Let me finish. What I mean is, that why is the body of the hijacker back there? I mean why was he in the rear of the plane? Wouldn't he have been with the pilot?"

"I didn't see him, but he must have rushed back to our section when he saw that the plane was going to crash," Marshal O'Connor said.

"Yeah, I remember seeing him, I think," John said. "But if that's the case, he should have a gun on him."

"He had," O'Connor said. "Mine."

"Your gun?" Desmond said.

"Yes. You see the stewardess came back and told me that Bennett already had my partner's gun and would kill him if I didn't hand mine over to her. I was to stay in my seat and not interfere."

"And you didn't?" John said incredulously.

"No. The important thing was to get the plane and passengers down safely in Montreal. Then we would deal with Bennett. So I handed my gun to the stewardess and she went off with it. Later I thought I heard shots from the front of the plane but I wasn't sure. I didn't know what to do. I didn't want to go up there and panic Bennett. Anyway, before I had a chance to do anything, we were coming down and the plane was coming apart."

"So you got your gun back?" Mark asked.

"Yes. Right after the crash I checked him out, and it was there. I have no idea what happened to my partner's gun," O'Connor sighed. "Poor Talmage . . ."

"Is it loaded?" Mark broke in.

"My gun? Yes." The marshal hesitated, then took the gun out of his pocket.

"Fantastic! Can John and I take it with us?" Mark reached out.

"Yeah, if you guys are depending on us to get you out of here, then we're going to need all the help we can get," John added. "With a gun we'd have a chance to kill something for food."

"Have either of you ever used a gun like this before?" O'Connor asked.

"No, but . . ." Mark began, and John was about to bluff it, when Mr. Lusty broke in.

"I think it could be a greater danger than help," he said.

"Right," the marshal hastily agreed. "Besides we'll need food, too, and there are four of us here."

"Okay, okay," John grudgingly gave in. "Let's get ready, Mark. I mean if we're going to go, the sooner the better." John got to his feet.

"I've been thinking about the food," Annie said. "I think you guys should get the sandwich for yourselves, and at least half of the candies. The rest of us will have to share the apple."

"Hey, that's not a fair split!" Desmond said. He felt a sudden secret gratification that he had eaten the other sandwich. They probably would have given both sandwiches to Mark and John.

"I know," Annie said. "But they'll be hiking all day. They'll need more energy than we will."

Mr. Lusty had already opened the box of candies and was counting them. "Sixty," he announced. He left half of the hard yellow, green, and blue candy balls in the box and made room for the sandwich beside them. Then he placed the box inside a knapsack Desmond and Annie had found. Also with the box went a rolled-up blanket taken from the plane.

Annie took several of the packs of matches she had found in the pockets of coats and gave some to Mark and some to John. "Better keep those in an inside pocket, where they won't get wet," she said.

Mark was struggling into a heavy flight jacket that had come from the plane. With a bit of squirming around, he was able to close the zipper all the way. Then Annie dug a lined topcoat out of the pile of clothing and gave it to John to wear over his light windbreaker.

In the meantime Mr. Lusty and Desmond had taken handfuls of paper out of briefcases and were handing them to the two boys.

"Shove these inside your clothes," Mr. Lusty said. "They'll help keep you warm and they'll be useful to start fires with."

"Do either of you have a knife?" Desmond asked.

"Yes, I have one," Mark said, pulling out a pocket-knife.

"Here. Take mine, too." Desmond said. "You never can tell."

Ten minutes later everyone was out in the middle of the clearing to see John and Mark leave. Annie impulsively hugged Mark, then John. "You guys be careful," she said, then stepped back.

"And remember, mine is a double cheeseburger and a chocolate malted," Desmond added.

Mr. Lusty shook hands with them both. "Take care of yourselves. I know you'll come through okay."

With John in the lead, both boys began to thread their way through the belt of young birch trees that grew on either side of the stream.

"Do you think they'll make it?" Annie asked, staring after them. Suddenly she felt very lonely and very lost.

No one answered.

6

"I'm freezing and I'm starving," John called.

Mark turned around. "C'mon huh, quit dragging all the time."

"I'm coming, I'm coming, don't lose your cool, man."

"Yeah, well, try and keep up, okay?" Mark grumbled.

"Yeah, sure. Listen, how many miles do you think we've come today?"

"Who knows? Ten? Twenty?"

"Don't you think we should stop for the night?" John asked.

"We still got at least an hour of daylight left."

"Well, I'm beat."

"We'll stop in a little while, okay?"

Roughly half an hour later John came to a large

boulder beside the stream and sat down in an attitude of collapse. Mark walked over and half sat, half leaned back against the chunk of granite. For a long moment both boys remained silent, with only the sound of their labored breathing to disturb the stillness.

Overhead the gray hanging sky held little light. Although the temperature was around the freezing mark, the boys were able to keep warm as long as they kept on the move. They generally felt the cold only when they stopped long enough for the sweat on their bodies to turn clammy, or when a particularly sharp gust of wind caught them out in an exposed area. Mainly though, the stream bed was sheltered from the wind.

"What time is it?" John asked.

"About six."

"Let's stop here for the night."

"Suits me."

"I'm tired. I'm not used to this kind of hiking," John said.

"Okay, we'll get a fire going."

"Yeah, my feet are sopping wet."

Mark looked around at the pine and fir trees that grew down the side of the draw. He was looking for a dead tree. He finally spotted one and went over to it and broke off some lower branches. They snapped off easily and he brought them back to the side of the stream.

"Over here," John said. He had found a spot along the bank of the stream where the water of a previous flood had carved out a shallow cave under the bank.

"We can sleep in here." He pointed to a flat piece of ground in front of the dirt cave. "And we can build our fire there."

John found a couple of dead trees along the stream and dragged their trunks back to the cave-like opening. He placed one on top of the other, crossing them slightly so that they would remain steady. Then he and Mark built a fire where the two trunks crossed. They crumpled up some pages from a magazine that Mark had stuffed inside his shirt and leaned small twigs against the balls of paper. Larger twigs were then braced in a teepee shape around the smaller ones.

"Ready?" Mark asked.

"Light her up!"

John scrambled to the other side of Mark and spread wide his topcoat to help block the wind. Mark lit the match and leaned forward. He touched off the paper and it quickly caught. They watched flames beneath one piece of paper form a glowing background to a color picture of a woman putting a roast turkey back inside the oven. The paper burned inward, the turkey gradually turning black. As they watched, the burned-to-a-crisp bird floated upward, breaking free of the fire, borne away on the night air to shatter into a hundred flakes of white ash against a low-hanging fir branch.

"There went our dinner," John said.

"Yeah," Mark agreed. "Listen, do you want to eat the sandwich now, or should we just have a candy and save the solid food for tomorrow?"

"Shoot, why not eat it now? I mean if that's all the food we got then it doesn't make much difference when we eat it. It's only got so many calories, right?"

"Psychologically it's better to ration it and make it last."

"You ration your half," John suggested. "I'm going to eat mine."

"Okay, so we eat it."

"We still have those candies for tomorrow and the next day," John pointed out. "And besides, we may find help by tomorrow."

Mark took out the sandwich, unwrapped it, and gave half to his companion. For ten minutes both boys were quiet as they munched their food. John ate his sandwich over a piece of paper, then carefully wet the tip of his middle finger and picked up, one by one, all the bread and cheese crumbs that had dropped.

"I wish I'd done that," Mark said.

"Every little bit counts."

"You know when I was a kid, I used never to eat the crusts on my sandwiches. Like I would leave two big 0's of crust on my plate."

"No kidding?"

"You know what I wish right now, don't you?"

"Yeah, you wish you had those crusts back again."

"Man, do I ever," Mark admitted. "Listen, what part of New York do you live in, John?"

"Harlem. Where you from?"

"Syracuse. Actually I live outside it, in a suburb."

"Which means you don't have any black kids in your school, right?"

"Sure we got black kids."

"Like how many? Ten? Five? Two?"

"About half a dozen."

"And how many kids in the whole school?" John asked.

"Around six hundred."

"Wow, you guys are really integrated."

"Yeah, okay, okay."

"We got a couple of whites in our school," John said.

"Yeah?"

"Yeah, the principal, the assistant principal, the guidance counselor."

Mark laughed, then said, "Hey, you know, I think we ought to gather more wood. This isn't enough to see us through the night."

"Okay, tell you what. We'll take turns. I'll go out and bring in a couple of armfuls and you watch the fire. Then you can go out and I'll watch the fire."

By the time dark fell they had gathered more than enough firewood to see them through until morning. Mark had taken off his shoes and was drying his stockings on a stick, holding them up in front of the heat. When both stockings were dry, he put them back on and then laid each shoe on its side, so that the openings faced the flames.

John took off his shoes and stockings and followed

Mark's example. "Hey, you know something strange?" he said. "My memory is still foggy. I can't remember the crash. I mean the actual moment of impact, or helping you get Mr. Lusty out of the plane."

"Do you remember looking out the window and seeing trees?"

"I can't be sure. I remember seein' a guy come down the aisle. Then the next thing I remember is I was helping you with the wounded guy, the hijacker."

"Just before we crashed, we both looked out the window. You said you saw trees. I thought I saw what looked like a mountain. Then we leaned back in our seats again and I started to say something when *kaboom!*—we hit. It'll all come back to you. Probably some sort of amnesia or shock or something."

"Yeah, I suppose. There's something weird about all this though. That guy saying his lawn mower was on the fritz."

"Hey, look you're starting to sound like Annie."

"Okay, okay. It's just damned weird is all." John rubbed his forehead. "Would you expect a dying bank robber to talk about his lawn mower?"

"Well no, but he did. So forget about it."

"Yeah, we got enough to worry about, I guess. What time you figure daylight comes in the morning?"

"Around seven I think."

"Which means we got about twelve hours," John said.

"About."

"I think we ought to take turns sleeping, so that one

guy can keep the fire going. What we can do is, I'll sleep from now to midnight. At midnight you wake me up and then you sleep until daylight."

"Okay."

John broke off the ends of some evergreen branches and spread them on the ground in front of the fire. Then he curled up in the blanket and tried to go to sleep. After ten minutes or so, he said, "Mark?"

"Yeah?"

"What does your father do?"

"He's a veterinarian. We got an animal hospital and he treats peoples' pets, mostly dogs and cats. How about your father?"

"Maintenance man in an office building in Manhattan. There's four of them. They fix doors that stick and water coolers that won't work and windows that jam— that sort of stuff."

"Sounds interesting."

"Fascinating, and he can advance all the way up to elevator operator someday," John laughed.

"What's so funny?"

"Listen, man, it's a big advancement. I mean you got to stop that elevator right even with the floor each time. It don't do to stop halfway between, or you just mess everybody up. Guy for the ninth floor, for example, he wouldn't know whether he was half a floor ahead of himself or half a floor behind."

"I see," Mark said doubtfully.

"You know, sometimes you're an awful pain in the dooadulum," John complained.

"Pain in the what?"

"Dooadulum."

"Never heard of it."

"You never heard of the dooadulum? Man, you're sure getting a deprived education in that fancy suburban school of yours."

"I think you made the word up," Mark said.

"Made it up? Come on, man, I wouldn't do a thing like that to a buddy. Okay, now look, I'm going to sleep and I don't want any wild animals sneaking up on me."

"I'll keep a good watch."

"Solid citizen man," John laughed. Then he pulled the blanket over his head.

At midnight, when Mark woke John, an inch of snow had already fallen.

7

"Oh brother, that's all we need." Desmond stood at the window, looking at the three-inch fall of snow that had come down during the night.

"That snow is going to cover up the wreck and they'll never find us now," Annie said.

"Never is a long time," Mr. Lusty said. He had been placed in charge of the box of candy balls and it had been agreed that they should have one apiece in the mornings and one apiece at night until there were no more candies left. Because of his gun and his competence with it, the marshal had been put in charge of hunting—scouting the nearby woods for possible game. So far he had had no luck. The apple had been split into quarters and eaten shortly after Mark and John left to get help.

Mr. Lusty passed around the box and Desmond took

the cellophane from around the candy and popped the hard yellow ball into his mouth.

"All right," Lusty called out. "We have to get organized. There are certain things we should be doing."

"Yeah, we could get busy and cook up some breakfast," Desmond said.

"We could all go outside," Lusty said. "Go out into the clearing and tramp out the letters S.O.S. in the snow."

"That's a terrific idea," Annie said.

"Sorry I can't help you," O'Connor said from his position in front of the fire. He lay on one side and patted his hip. "That trip out this morning did me in. This hip is sore. I can hardly move it."

"That's okay," Desmond said. "We'll do it."

Mr. Lusty and the two young people went outside. The sky had cleared and the sun was shining directly overhead, cheering them with its warmth and its promise of search planes. Under the old man's supervision, Desmond and Annie tramped out the S.O.S. sign. An hour later the three giant letters were beaten carefully into the white snow.

When Desmond and Annie came back to the fire, they took off their shoes. Their toes were semi-frozen from cold and wet. A towel, one of several salvaged from the plane, was passed around to dry off their feet, and stockings were soon being held up to the flames. Wisps of steam rose from the wet wool. No sooner had they gotten their stockings and shoes dry, when Desmond heard a faint, far-away throbbing sound. "What's that?" He cocked his head.

The others strained to listen.

"A plane!" Desmond jumped to his feet and rushed outside, followed by Annie and Mr. Lusty. They danced and waved their arms and shouted over and over but the tiny white dot sailed majestically along, drawing twin contrail plumes ruler straight across the sky.

"How high is he, do you think?" Desmond said.

"Thirty thousand feet," Lusty replied.

"You think they can see our sign?" Annie asked.

"Probably not," Mr. Lusty admitted.

"You mean you let us jump around here for nothing?" Desmond asked.

"You can never be sure. They won't all be flying that high," Lusty said. "Anyway, for at least a couple of minutes there you had some hope. That's important."

"Yeah, and got our feet sopping wet all over again for nothing," Desmond said.

Dispirited, they trooped back into the cabin.

"Didn't see us, huh?" The marshal turned from his position by the fire.

"No, too high." Desmond sat down and began to take off his shoes. They had now been marooned three days and the lack of food was beginning to affect them, especially Desmond and Annie whose still-growing bodies used up more energy. Annie sometimes felt lightheaded when she stood up, or made any sort of abrupt move. In addition to the pain in his side, Desmond suffered from periodic stomach cramps, sharp tearing pains that made him more and more irritable. And if that weren't enough, he seemed to be catching a cold.

"You know, I just thought of something," Mr. Lusty said. "Annie, do you have a mirror?"

"Yes, in my flight bag." Annie opened her flight bag and took out a small rectangular mirror about the size of a playing card.

"Good. Anyone else have a mirror? We can use them to flash signals to airplanes."

"I know what we can use, the bottom of the drinking bowl." Annie pointed to the half-full, stainless steel bowl. "I can empty out the water and use the bottom. It's nice and shiny."

"Yes." Mr. Lusty laid the mirror on the table. "Now if we hear another plane, Desmond you grab the mirror and Annie you get the bowl and we'll try to signal the pilot."

"You guys are dreaming," the marshal said. "That only happens in movies."

The old man ignored the marshal's comment. The man's attitude was beginning to bother him. Though he went out hunting every day, he was never gone very long, and he refused to let anyone go with him and he wouldn't let anyone else use or borrow his gun. Mr. Lusty idly picked up the coil of copper wire Desmond had earlier taken from the plane. He'd do some hunting of his own. It had been sixty years, maybe even more, since his father had shown him how to make a rabbit snare. Still he was almost sure he could remember the mechanics of it. You shaped the piece of wire into a running noose. Then the rabbit came hopping along, the head and neck went through the open noose, and the driving weight of the animal's body caused the wire to pull tight. The other end of the wire was tied to a stake driven into the ground.

Mr. Lusty got to his feet, put the wire in his pocket, and said, "Going out for a minute. I'll bring some firewood back."

He thought he'd seen some tracks when he was outside earlier in the day, helping with the S.O.S. sign. He walked across to the far end of the clearing, to the top of the first S. they had trampled out. Yes, there they were, plain as day, a set of small round pads.

He slipped on his glasses, crouched down, and held the noose above the tracks. The copper wire gleamed in the sun. The whole snare would be too obvious out in the open, he thought. He followed the tracks into some undergrowth, into a tunnel of high grass and low bush that outlined what was obviously a well-used rabbit trail. What was it his father had said? Rabbits were such creatures of habit that not only did they keep using the same trail over and over again, they hopped on exactly the same spots on the trail so that a rabbit trail was a series of worn grass pads, each about the size of a silver dollar.

Then too the wire was supposed to be rubbed with a pellet of rabbit dung picked up on the same trail. This was to hide the human scent. Also the anchor stake in the ground had to be completely hidden with grass or leaves, and the same thing done with the set-up stake. It was incredible how it all came back to him. He could remember when he was twelve or thirteen, cycling into town with half a dozen dead rabbits tied together by their front paws, their furry bodies looped over the handlebars of the machine. He got a nickel apiece for them from old Dutch Honiger who, for some mysterious reason, also bought empty burlap bags for a penny apiece. He hadn't thought of Dutch Honiger for fifty years, not since the day he got the letter from his father saying that the old rag and bone trader had been run over by a farm tractor.

He broke a small Y-shaped branch off a fir tree and cut a stake from it. Working slowly and carefully he sharpened a point on the stake and tied the end of the snare wire just beneath the Y so that the wire could not pull off. With a large rock he managed to pound the stake into the semi-frozen ground about a foot to one side of the trail. He then cut a smaller stake and notched one end into a V-shape, in the groove of which he laid the single wire running from the anchor stake. This smaller support stake propped the stiff wire of the snare about three or four inches above the trail. The open loop now yawned over the trail and he tilted it slightly to make sure that it was perpendicular to the ground. The loop was supposed to be one hand high above the trail. Any lower and the rabbit might jump on top of the loop, any higher and the animal might brush under it.

The old man stood back to admire his work, quite pleased with himself. It looked fine, he thought, but there was one thing more to do. With the tip of a fir branch, he carefully brushed the snow over both stakes until they were completely hidden. Then he walked backwards, brushing out his footsteps as he retreated.

As he detoured over to the woodpile, he decided to say nothing about his snare. Maybe it would be better not to get everyone's hopes up until he had something definite to show them.

He picked up one piece of firewood and looked at the remaining dozen or so wedges of split wood. They had hardly enough to last until tomorrow. He would have to get someone to forage for fuel if they were to keep a fire going.

8

Both boys lurched to a halt where the creek joined another creek of similar size, forming a much larger stream. Mark removed his gloves and blew on his hands, then reached into an inside pocket and took out a pencil. With a fresh piece of paper, he drew a Y to represent the juncture of the two creeks. He drew an arrow pointing up the right leg of the Y.

"What are you doing?" John asked, looking over Mark's shoulder.

"Making a map, in case someone has to come back this way." Mark folded the piece of paper and replaced it in an inside pocket. "There will probably be other junctures and we won't always remember which fork we took. A rescue party might want to hike back in, and this way they got a route to follow."

"Yeah." John looked down at his shoes. "My feet

are soaked again. That snow last night sure didn't help any."

"I know. It was just enough to keep our feet wet all day."

"How many miles do you think we've come since morning?" John asked.

"I don't know, what difference does it make?"

"I'd just like to know is all."

Mark checked his watch. "It's one o'clock now and we started out at six—that's seven hours. Say two miles an hour. Fourteen miles?"

"You'd think in fourteen miles we'd run across something; a house, or a road, or even some lousy telephone lines."

"Yeah, it's not exactly encouraging," Mark admitted. "Trouble with following the creek is that our visibility is limited, down in a draw like this, with nothing but trees all around."

"Yeah, we could pass within a hundred feet of a house and not see it." John slipped on an icy patch of ground. He lost his balance and fell to one knee. For a moment he remained motionless, looking ahead to where Mark was trying to find a way around a heavy clump of snow-laden thorn bushes that overhung the stream. Painfully John pushed himself upright, got to his feet, brushed the snow off his legs, and moved ahead. "Hey, Mark!"

"Yeah?" Mark detoured up the slope of the draw to work around the thorn bushes. John followed him.

"Listen, Mark, I heard of guys like you before, but I

thought they only lived in Hollywood or on television. I mean planning to spend the summer in Europe on your own. Don't you think you ought to break in on some easy place like Staten Island before you tackle Europe?"

"Ah, Europe's nothing," Mark said. "Anyway I been there before, when I was fifteen."

"On your own?"

"No, part of a tour. About twenty of us went over one Easter. Our French teacher was in charge of us."

"Okay, now tell me again, how much money are you going to need?"

"Four hundred dollars. Two hundred for the plane and two hundred for living expenses."

"No way, man. You can't live two months in Europe on two hundred dollars," John argued. "And don't forget you got to buy a bicycle out of that. A new bike cost you fifty to a hundred."

Mark ducked his head and waddled underneath the low branches of a spruce. "Second-hand, I'll pick one up for twenty bucks, tops."

"Okay, but how about hotels and food?"

"I'll stay in youth hostels every night, only fifty cents for a bed. And they have stoves and everything you can cook on, and I'll buy bread and baloney and fruit in little stores along the way and make my own meals."

"And where are you going to get the money, your folks?"

"No, I'm going to sell my shares in the investment club in school."

"You mean shares of stock—like on Wall Street?"

"Yeah. When we were freshmen a bunch of us started an investment club. It's kind of like a mutual fund. You know what a mutual fund is?"

"I heard of them, but not really."

"Well, anyway, we pool our money and buy and sell stock in different companies as a way of investing."

"So how has it worked out?"

"Oh, we made a little money," Mark laughed. "About what we could have made if we had put the money in the bank in the first place. Anyway, I sure learned a lot about the stock market and how it works."

John fell silent. Mark was beginning to impress him. Okay, so he looked like your typical spoiled white suburban kid who had it made, with no worries about anything. But there was more to him than you would figure. For one thing he never tried to put you down. And he was a lot tougher than John figured he would be. So far there hadn't been a word of complaint out of him—he certainly wasn't a crybaby, you had to give him that.

Somewhere below him Mark was calling. John was dog-tired but he tried to quicken his pace. Eventually he caught up with his companion and they emerged from the brushy walls of the draw to where the stream leveled out and meandered away through a large flat meadow.

"Looks like easy going for a while," Mark said.

Ahead of them spread a large flat frozen surface, with here and there a tuft of dried grass sticking above the snow.

"Don't count on it," John warned. "That looks sort of mushy ahead of us.

And indeed the meadow turned out to be a marsh that was almost impossible to cross. The boys did manage to move ahead and follow the stream for a few yards but Mark soon broke through the frozen skin of ice and snow and sank to his shins in mud. He got out of the hole and retreated, then tried a different approach. Again he broke through and this time John had to help pull him out.

"We gotta bypass this place somehow," Mark said, staring down at his mud-covered legs.

They retraced their steps and cut back into the woods, swinging out to their left a couple of hundred yards. Then they tried to work through the trees and brush in the general direction the stream had been flowing, parallel to its course.

A couple of hours later they had bypassed the marsh and picked up the stream again. Both boys were now exhausted and barely able to keep moving. But even resting was painful. After a minute or so the cold would get through to them and they would begin to shiver, so that it was less painful to keep staggering along, tired as they were.

Along toward late afternoon the creek again broke out of the woods as it plunged in steep ten-foot drops down the side of a mountain. Before they began their descent the boys looked down the sheer rock slabs. Here and there showers of spray leaped high in the air as the body of water fell through space to crash on a rocky ledge.

Mark shook his head. "Wow, we're going to have to be careful along here."

"Yeah. One slip and your neck bone is no longer connected to your head bone."

"Listen, why don't we stop here for the night and tackle this slope in the morning?"

"I don't know. I don't think it's a good place to spend the night," John pointed out. "There's no shelter from the wind and not much wood around for a fire."

"Look, you see that big tree?" Mark pointed to a large spruce that grew on an exposed ridge some fifty feet away.

"Okay, let's one of us climb that tree and see if we can spot anything," John agreed.

They set off for the tree. With a leg up from John, Mark was able to reach the lowest branch and haul himself up.

"Be careful," John called up to him. "You see anything?"

"Naw, just woods." Mark climbed a bit higher, looked all around, then came down. "Not a sign of anything." He dropped to the ground.

"Oh boy, and I was sure you'd spot a McDonalds or a Kentucky Fried Chicken."

"Yeah, well," Mark managed a chuckle. "There could be all kinds of goodies out there, but in those woods you wouldn't notice them."

"Okay, let's first get down this steep part. At the bottom we should find plenty of firewood," John said.

"Fine, but let's stick together in case one of us slips or falls or something."

They angled back toward the creek and the drop-off.

71 —

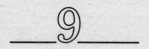

9

Mr. Lusty was quite impressed with himself. The frozen rabbit lay on its side, four legs stiff. The snow had been trampled down in a circle all around the stake. The terrified animal had kept trying to leap and buck its way free but the stake held firm and each jump had only tightened the wire around the rabbit's neck until finally its breathing was cut off.

Carefully easing down, the old man crouched over the small animal and dug his fingers into the fur of its neck, feeling for the snare wire. He managed to get one finger under the wire and pull open the noose. Sliding the wire off over the head, he picked up the rabbit by its hind legs and held the frozen carcass aloft. For a moment he felt a stab of pity for the creature as he brushed the snow off its fur. But then he thought of the others in the cabin.

The rabbit weighed maybe a pound, he thought. Enough for a snack for the four of them. At least there was one good thing in being seventy-five. You no longer felt hunger the way young people did. In fact, many people his age had to be reminded to eat.

On his way back to the cabin, he stopped every once in a while to look for more tracks. His search was rewarded when he picked up another set of pads beside a fallen log. He would teach Desmond and Annie how to set out snares. With any luck they would soon have more rabbit meat for the pot.

The old man opened the door of the cabin and swung the rabbit aloft.

"Well, I'll be darned!" the marshal quietly said.

"Wow!" Annie exclaimed.

"A rabbit," Desmond said, then began to cough. Desmond's cold had gotten much worse and his bouts of coughing seemed to last longer and longer.

Mr. Lusty laid the rabbit out on the table. Marshal O'Connor limped over and poked it with his forefinger.

"I can't believe it," Annie said. "Real food!"

"We can barbecue it in the fireplace," O'Connor said.

"No, no," Lusty said. "There's only one way to cook it. Cut it up and make soup of it. Barbecueing is too wasteful. We'll get every ounce of nourishment if we turn it into soup."

"How did you catch it?" Annie asked.

Mr. Lusty held up the wire snare. "With this." He

explained that his father had once taught him how to set out snares and catch rabbits.

"That's fantastic," Desmond coughed. "Are there any more rabbits out there?"

"Yes, I think so."

"I'll clean him." The marshal took out a large pocket-knife and opened the rabbit's stomach. Reaching inside the cavity, he pulled forth all the guts.

"Separate out the heart and lungs, the liver and the kidneys and keep them for the pot," Mr. Lusty said.

Annie brought the stainless steel bowl over to the table. The marshal dumped the edible organs into the water, then began to skin the rabbit. He cut a circle in the fur just above each paw, then peeled the fur back until each leg came cleanly into view. Starting then with a cut under the tail, he pulled back on the fur until the whole outer skin came smoothly away over the rabbit's head.

"Cut it all up into tiny pieces, as tiny as you can get them," Mr. Lusty directed.

It took the marshal half an hour to get the rabbit minced up and into the pot. The animal's bones were broken into small pieces so that the marrow would melt out and become part of the soup. The marshal even scraped the inside of the fur with the blade of his knife and put the fat scrapings into the pot. Finally the rabbit stew was ready and the pot placed on some coals.

Soon a faint smell of broth began to tease everyone's nose. Mr. Lusty insisted that they keep the rabbit boiling until the meat was ready to fall apart. Finally the pot was taken out of the fireplace and allowed to cool for a while. Then the old man picked up one of the wax paper cups to use as a measure. Each person got a full cup of soup, with tiny pieces of meat and bone floating around in it.

Annie's face wore an expression of intense pleasure as she blew on the fragrant soup, then tried a sip from the cup. "Oooh, oooh, this tastes so good I can hardly stand it."

Desmond leaned back against the wall of the hut and closed his eyes. "Good? It's so good I could cry." Desmond's cold had taken its toll of his strength. His eyes were bright and feverish and his cheeks, despite the four-day stubble of blond beard, had a sunken look. He took another sip. "I have never, never, never in my life tasted anything as good as this."

"Delicious," Annie agreed.

"Who's ready for seconds?" Lusty asked.

There was enough soup in the pot to give everyone two full cups each. The half cup that was left over after the second distribution was given to Desmond at Annie's insistence because of his fever.

In the meantime Mr. Lusty had retrieved the rest of the copper wire and was busy fashioning new snares. "When I finish these," he said to Annie, "perhaps you and the marshal will come out and watch while I set them."

"Sure," Annie agreed, touching the bridge of her nose, gingerly.

"It looks much better," Mr. Lusty said.

The swelling had gone down around Annie's eyes and nose, though the skin was still badly discolored.

"It still hurts when I touch it," she said.

The marshal patted his hip. "My hip is still not working right," he said. "I'd like to help you set those snares, but I don't think it will support me."

Desmond was silent. He wanted to help, but he was scared of what was happening to him. He was afraid that he had begun to imagine things. Last night he thought he saw Mark bending over the fire. He had almost called out to him. He felt lightheaded all the time and he had stopped worrying about whether they would be rescued or not. He had to concentrate more. But it was hard with that pain in his ribs. Maybe he was being punished for eating that sandwich, maybe that was it. Now what were they arguing about?

"That's too long," Marshal O'Connor said.

Annie held up her length of wire and looked at it. "What difference does it make?"

"If you make them too long," O'Connor said, "we won't get as many snares out of the wire."

Mr. Lusty got to his feet. "Let's go outside and set the ones we've made, Annie."

"Can I help?" Desmond asked.

"No, you stay there at the fire," Lusty said. "Annie and I will manage just fine."

"What's that?" Annie said suddenly, opening the door. "Listen, that sound . . ."

They all strained to listen. Then Desmond insisted on getting up and going outside with them. The two young

people and the old man stood in the middle of the clearing for a good five minutes, searching the skies and listening for aircraft.

But it turned out to be another busted hope, another
ghost aircraft that couldn't be seen and even now was
no longer to be heard.

10

"What is it?" John asked. It was early afternoon and both boys were face to face with a small brown furry animal that had approached the creek for a drink.

"A bear cub!" Mark said, shuffling out of his knapsack and letting it drop to the ground.

John squatted down on his haunches and began calling to the bear. The cub sat down twenty yards away and whimpered.

"Here little squirt, come here," John said, putting out his hand.

Mark looked around for a large stone or stick.

The bear cub whimpered as John called again, "Here boy, here boy."

The cub tumbled closer, then sat down again and gave another whimper. At that moment something began thrashing around in the nearby undergrowth. There was an explosion of parting branches and a large bear shot out and into the open.

"Climb a tree!" Mark shouted as soon as he caught sight of the animal. The bear had another cub galloping at her heels. When the bear reached her lost infant, she stopped to sniff him all over, giving the boys enough time to scramble up some nearby trees.

John managed to get fifteen feet up a young spruce tree, where he sat down gingerly on a branch. Below him the large mother bear was angrily whuffing and snuffling and clawing at the dirt. Every once in a while she would reach up and hit the trunk of the tree a cuff with her paw, trying to knock John loose.

John held onto the trunk with both hands. The tree was actually swaying back and forth with the force of the blows. Disappointed that she couldn't jar her enemy loose, the bear went over to the tree in which Mark was roosting. In between angry roars she batted the trunk of Mark's tree while Mark held on for dear life. The trunks of the young spruce trees were too thin for the bear to grasp and climb. Finally the animal tired of her attack and wandered off. The knapsack drew her attention. John watched her sniff the sack, then cuff it with one paw. The canvas bag flew up into the air and landed on top of some nearby bushes. Fortunately the box of hard candies remained inside.

"Mark?"

"Yeah?"

"You okay?"

"I'll be okay as soon as I stop shivering."

"Man, that animal isn't very friendly, is she?"

"No she isn't," Mark agreed. "I almost trampled this tree into the ground I was in such a hurry to get up here."

"Yeah, I know what you mean. I thought I was tired until I saw that thing coming for me. Where is she? Can you see her?"

"No. Maybe I'll go down and look around," Mark said.

"Yeah, me too."

"No, you stay up there as a lookout." Mark began a slow descent of his tree. He reached the last branch and, after a careful glance around, dropped to the ground. He could see the tracks of the animal leading off into some heavy brush. There were several fresh gouge marks at his feet, where the bear had slashed at the dirt in frustration.

"You see anything?" Mark called.

"No, no sign of her anywhere."

Mark relaxed and walked over to the foot of John's tree. He stood there for a moment, examining the freshly raked claw marks on the bark. Then he looked up at his companion. "I guess you can come down now."

The words were no sooner out of his mouth when he heard two things: the sound of something crashing through brush and John's warning cry, "Look out, here she comes again!"

Mark jumped straight up, caught a branch, and shinnied his way to John's outstretched hand.

Once again the bear was batting the trunk, causing the whole tree to shiver violently. Halfway up, arms around the trunk, both boys grimly hung on.

For the next hour or so, until it grew dark, the bear would periodically wander off and the boys would discuss coming down. However, as soon as one of them started to descend, the bear would reappear and begin to whack and cuff the trunk with her paw. After a while she would tire of her game and shuffle away. Her cubs were not with her and the boys guessed that she had them hidden safely away in some nearby brush or cave.

"That animal's never gonna let us down," John said.

"She'll probably take her cubs and move away tonight sometime."

"Yeah, but I'm not about to go down to find out if she's still hanging around, not in the dark."

"Looks like we might have to stay up here until morning," Mark agreed. "At least we're both in the same tree."

"Beautiful, man," John said. "I tell you I don't think I can last the night. I don't have the strength to hang on."

"Yes, you do," Mark argued. "Hey, you notice it seems to be warming up a bit? It's not as cold as it was."

John shifted around on the branch. "Thing is, I can't get comfortable," he complained.

"Yeah, I know. Tell you what, let's plan the first meal we're going to have after we're rescued."

"Naw, I'm tired of that," John said. "You tell me about your trip to England. And if you work a little food into the story, why that's okay."

"All right. But you've got to go too, but no elaborate meals."

"Okay. It's a deal. And no fancy banquets, just lunch-counter stuff," John said. "Where we at, Kennedy?"

"Right. We've checked our luggage and they've looked at our tickets and passports and we have our boarding cards."

"How long until the plane takes off?"

"Oh, we got an hour yet," Mark said. "Right now we're wandering around looking for a place to buy some English money."

"Oh yeah. How much money are we carrying?"

"Two hundred dollars apiece."

"Okay, go ahead."

"So we go into the foreign currency store and we exchange twenty dollars for English pounds."

"Okay, and how many pounds is that?"

"Let's see." Mark was silent for a moment. "Probably about eight pounds, eleven pence."

"Okay. Listen, how are you carrying your American money? You got a checkbook or what?"

"I've got it all in twenty dollar travelers' checks."

"Okay. Well, I got mine in cash, in a money belt around my waist."

"Hey man, that's real square. Nobody carries a money belt any more," Mark said.

"This dude does. Anyway I always wanted to wear a money belt. All right, go ahead. We're getting our English money. Hey, if we're going to be in England so long, how come we're only changing twenty dollars?"

"Because the rate of exchange will probably be better in England. We should be able to get more for our dollars over there."

"I see. Okay, go ahead."

"Well, we got a problem now," Mark pointed out. "We still have forty-five minutes to kill and we each got a couple of dollars' worth of small change in our pockets. Now the American small change won't be any good in England, so we have to use it up. We can go to a newsstand and buy a bunch of magazines and candy bars . . ."

"Yeah?"

"Or we can go to the cafeteria and order a hamburger, our last American hamburger for three months."

"Whoa, wait a minute," John said. "Exactly how much small change have we got?"

"You count your own. I've got two dollars, two twenty-five, two thirty, and five pennies—two thirty-five altogether."

"Well, I got two seventy-five, exactly eleven quarters."

"Ah come on," Mark objected. "You mean you don't have any nickels or dimes or even a few pennies?"

"Shoot man, I told you, exactly eleven quarters. That's the way it turned out, all quarters."

"Okay, so what do you want to do with your money?"

"I'm going to the newsstand. I'm going to buy a Baby Ruth and a Mason peppermint bar."

"Okay, that's fifty cents say. What are you going to do with the rest of your change?"

"Well, how much does a burger with all the trimmings cost in the cafeteria?"

"You want cheese on it?"

"Yeah, and with a milk shake."

"Okay, and you want like, two slices of pickles, right?"

"Yeah, pickles."

"And one of those delicious buns with crunchy seeds on top?"

"That's right."

"And French fries? A big handful of thick, crisp, golden French fries, right?" Mark asked.

"Oh man yes, French fries, absolutely gotta have French fries."

"Okay, and you want one of those little paper cups of cole slaw, right?"

"Um yes, that's right, drowning in mayonnaise."

"And a slice of tomato and a couple of fresh, crisp lettuce leaves?"

"Right," John said in a dreaming yet anguished voice.

"Yeah, well that all comes to two fifteen."

"Fantastic. I got a dime left over."

For a little while there was silence, except for the sporadic clash and rustle of pine needles as a breeze hopscotched through the evergreens. Then John broke the quiet. "Mark?"

"Yeah?"

"I see you're not eating your pickle."

"Well, I'm not exactly crazy for pickles. You want it?"

"Thanks. Man, I love pickles."

"Listen, I think that's us," Mark called.

"What?"

Mark's voice changed to a higher key as he imitated the precise voice and polished diction of a flight announcer. "Your attention please. TWA flight one one seven, New York to London, is now boarding at Gate 17. Will passengers proceed to Gate 17? Please have your boarding passes ready."

"That's us, huh?"

"Right."

"Mark?"

"Yeah?"

"That was a great hamburger. I'll always remember it."

"Yeah, me too," Mark agreed.

"We on the plane yet?"

"Going up the steps."

"Right. Now look, how many meals do we get on the plane?"

"Well, just after we take off, I think we get dinner.

85 __

Then about an hour before we land in London, we should get breakfast."

"Wow, man, two big meals in the next six hours."

"That's right. Okay, we're at the end of the runway now, waiting for clearance."

"Listen, Mark?"

"Yeah?"

"I'm afraid of falling asleep up here."

"You won't. Tell you what, I'll take off my belt and we'll tie ourselves together. Then if one of us starts to nod off, he'll warn the other one."

"Okay."

Mark worked around on the branch until he had his belt taken off. He ran the belt through one of the loops on his trousers and gave the other end of the belt to John. John pushed the tongue of Mark's belt through the buckle of his own belt and notched it in. He gave a tug and grunted with satisfaction.

"Now if one of us falls, we both fall," Mark said.

"Yeah man, I can see us hanging on each side of a low branch and that bear going crazy trying to decide which one of us to start on first."

For some reason the comment struck Mark funny and he began to laugh. Soon the woods were ringing with their laughter. After a while, though, the laughter died down and silence fell as they grimly prepared to wait out the long night.

11

Desmond pulled the blanket tight around his shoulders. He managed to control a fit of shivering long enough to ask, "What day is it?"

"Day? Monday? Sunday?" Annie asked.

Mr. Lusty, sitting on the pine boughs in front of the fire, carefully turned around and reached under the table for the briefcase. He pulled it to him and opened it on his lap. Pulling out a clipboard, he turned over half a dozen pages of a legal pad and announced, "Monday, March 29. Day 8. Snares O. Hunting O. First complete day without food of any kind." He raised his head and looked around at the others.

"What good is all that scribbling going to do us?" Marshal O'Connor angrily asked.

"If we don't make it, at least there will be a record of

how long we lasted," Lusty replied. "I happen to think we've done quite well so far."

"*You* happen to think," O'Connor said disgustedly. "Another thing, will you quit your fidgeting! Between you and your fidgets and Desmond and his coughing, nobody can get any rest around here."

"I'm sorry," the older man said.

"We're not going to make it, you know," Desmond calmly informed the others.

"Yes, we will," Annie said.

"You'd think those two would have reached help by now," O'Connor said.

"Maybe they did, maybe help is on the way in to us," Lusty said.

"Maybe the moon is made of green cheese," O'Connor snorted.

"Without food they couldn't last more than a week," Desmond argued. "Add another two days to get help back in to us."

"So?" Annie said.

"So if we're not rescued by tomorrow, or the day after, then forget about it. It means Mark and John never made it out," Desmond argued. "It means they're lying dead somewhere."

"You can never be sure, perhaps they found food on the way," Mr. Lusty said.

"I know one thing. I'm hungry," Desmond said.

"You've said that a thousand times already, put a sock on it," the marshal grumbled.

"We could boil up those rabbit bones again and try another run of rabbit soup," Mr. Lusty said.

"What's the use, it still comes out water in the end," the marshal said.

"I thought sure we'd get another rabbit," Desmond said. "I mean we've got eight snares out there."

"Maybe you kids are doing something wrong," Marshal O'Connor said.

"I don't see what," Annie argued. "We're doing it just the way Mr. Lusty showed us. Besides, I don't know how you can complain. You haven't contributed a thing and you've got a gun!"

"Now, now, the snares look fine." Mr. Lusty tried to cool things down. "Maybe there was only one rabbit out there to begin with. There haven't been any more tracks in the clearing and the marshal certainly hasn't seen any out in the woods."

"There are plenty of blue jays out there. Maybe the marshal could shoot one with his gun," Desmond said sarcastically.

"Talk sense. Even if I hit one, there'd be nothing left but feathers."

"Oh dear Lord," Annie prayed. "Send a big moose, with poor eyesight and lots of feathers and have him break his neck on our doorstep."

"Send even a small moose," Desmond added.

"Cut the funny stuff," O'Connor shouted. "You kids know if I'd seen anything out there I'd have shot it. I'm just as hungry as you are."

Desmond slowly got to his feet. For a moment he steadied himself with one hand pressing back against the wall. "Okay, Annie," he finally said. "We need more wood. Let's see what we can dig up."

The two young people left the cabin and started to cross the clearing.

"Our sign has practically disappeared," Desmond pointed out.

"Yes. That rain last night really melted it fast."

All that remained of the original S.O.S. were three snowball-sized clumps of snow, the three periods after the three letters.

They continued across the clearing. "This was probably a trapper or a prospector's cabin once," Desmond said. "And this meadow was probably pasture for his horse."

"Too bad he didn't have a little garden somewhere."

"He probably did," Desmond said. "But it would have gone right back to the wild the first year he abandoned the place."

Desmond bent over to examine a snare. Still nothing. Eight snares, eight nothings. They had been lucky the first time, but since then not a sign, not even tracks in the soft mud patches that bordered the creek. Were he and Annie doing something wrong with the snares? Or had the warmer weather somehow broadcast the human scent and now the rabbits were staying away from the clearing? Or had there really been only one rabbit to begin with?

They began to work their way into the woods, looking for dead timber and fallen branches. They halted at one deadfall, but trying to lift it sent Desmond into a vicious spasm of coughing. He had to sit down for a moment or so until he got his breathing back to normal.

"You're all blue in the face," Annie said. "You're trying to do too much."

Desmond shook his head. "No," he managed to get out.

"You just help me find the wood," Annie said. "I'll carry it back."

Desmond nodded. "My lungs feel as heavy as a bag of wet sand."

"That's that cold of yours."

For the next fifteen minutes or so, Desmond restricted himself to building small piles of dead branches here and there for Annie to collect later on. In the meantime Annie was foraging for heavier wood and finally came back to Desmond dragging a long, dead tree trunk.

"You look like a picture in my geography book," Desmond said.

"Your geography book?"

"Yeah. All you need is a scarf around your head and you're one of the pictures in the middle of the book—Old Carpathian Peasant Bringing Home the Firewood." Desmond managed a weak grin.

"Why thanks," Annie responded. "That's very sweet of you. You just made my day."

"Only kidding," Desmond said. "Actually you've been the best one of us all, you know."

"I'm not as badly hurt as the rest of you," Annie said.

"You still think we'll be rescued?"

"Of course. The wreckage is bound to be discovered pretty soon."

"Well, maybe," Desmond conceded. He lifted an armful of kindling sticks and followed Annie as she dragged the dead log across the clearing.

"Our S.O.S. sign is all melted away," Annie reported as they entered the cabin.

"You know I was thinking about that," Lusty said. "Actually we don't need snow. We can use the tips of evergreen branches. The dark green will stand out quite nicely against the tan of the dead grass."

"But won't the wind blow the branches all over the place?" Desmond asked.

"We can anchor the branches with stones from the bed of the creek."

"Okay," Annie said with a sudden burst of enthusiasm. "Let's have our midday cup of rabbit water and then, Desmond, you and I can spend the afternoon gathering branches and making a new sign."

"You're wasting your time on those signs," O'Connor said.

"Well, that's one thing we have plenty of, isn't it?" Annie said.

12

"Mark?"

"Yeah?"

"You sleeping?"

"What are you, crazy?" Mark demanded. "I'm not an ape. I can't sleep sitting on a branch thirty feet above the ground."

"Listen, you listening?"

"No, I'm sleeping."

"Something keeps bothering me about the crash. It keeps going round and round in my head."

"Look, quit worrying about it. We crashed, that's all. There were shocks and noise and smoke."

"Yeah, but what did I do?" John asked. "Was there someone crying, saying, 'Oh God, oh God' over and over?"

"Yes, there was. I think it might have been the hijacker. And then you and me went to the back of the plane and helped old Mr. Lusty.''

"Yeah, it's coming back to me. I sort of remember noise and confusion and a coat over my head.''

"You remember your seat belt?'' Mark asked.

"My seat belt?''

"Yeah, you went to loosen it and the whole thing came away in your hand.''

John got excited. "Yeah, now I remember. And there was an umbrella sticking out of one of the seats in front of us.''

"That's right.''

"And just before the plane crash, a man came hurrying down the aisle.''

"That was the hijacker.''

"Yeah. No, wait a minute. If that was the hijacker, then the man who was moaning had to be someone else. Because I remember that the moaning sound came from in front of me, and the man who came down the aisle went on past my seat—to the rear of the plane.''

"So what difference does it make?''

"I dunno . . . but I . . .''

"Look, the sky is beginning to lighten,'' Mark interrupted. The visibility was slowly but steadily improving. Mark could now see the creek bed, despite wisps of fog, ten to twenty yards into the trees. "Should we chance it?'' he asked.

"Yeah, let's get down out of here,'' John said. "That animal is probably gone.''

"I sure hope so."

"I'll go first." John began to lower himself and in a minute or so was standing beneath the tree. "I'll scout around a bit. You wait," John called.

Cautiously he moved into the trees, letting out a shout every once in a while to give the bear plenty of warning. But their tormentor of the night before had evidently fled the scene. He retrieved the knapsack, then called Mark down from his perch. Soon both boys had their shoes off and were warming their feet in front of a fire. Finally they got their footgear thoroughly dry, put out the fire, and were able to resume following the stream bed.

For the rest of the morning their trek was uneventful except for one ten-minute period when a large black bird followed them and kept up a constant scolding. The bird flitted from branch to branch ahead of them, chattering away. They tried to hit the bird with stones and pieces of wood, but it seemed to lead a charmed life. Finally, after a last-minute burst of chatter, the bird flew off and did not return.

At mid-day they halted for a break. There was little change in the character of the land they were hiking over. It was mile after mile of forest, though the trees might change from birch to pine to fir and back to birch again. The stream was twice as broad as it had been when they had started out, and it was no longer easy to cross from one bank to the other when they found the way blocked by some obstacle. Now they sometimes had to make wide detours around large patches of chin-high thorny brush before they could pick up the trail again.

Once, for a period of an hour, they lost the river completely when they made a detour. They finally had to backtrack and try another way around the fifty-foot waterfall that had stopped them. Usually, no matter how close or far away the stream was, they could hear the water splashing off boulders and sometimes, when the course was steep, the constant dull rumble of boulders being bowled along the stream bed by the velocity of the water.

It was mid-afternoon and both boys were staggering. They had had almost no sleep the night before and were bone tired. They were using crude walking sticks now to help them over the rough spots. In fact Mark was so tired that when he saw a furry-looking creature on their path a few yards ahead of him, he politely waited for the animal to move on. It was a porcupine. Its thousands of black quills were tipped with silver, and its broad triangular flat paddle of a tail dragged behind the waddling animal like a miniature doormat.

Brought up short, John asked, "What is it?"

"Porcupine."

As though aware that it was the center of attention, the animal stopped.

"Can you eat it?" John asked.

"I think so."

"Then kill it with your stick, man!"

The porcupine, sensing danger, had curled up into a

ball, its color changing from black to gray as it presented a thousand silver-tipped quills to its enemy. For a moment Mark hesitated. Then he lifted his stick and brought it down as hard as he could on the animal's back. The porcupine quivered once and its fur seemed to ripple as the animal tightened up even harder to become a bristling ball of miniature spears that defied the world.

Now both boys were battering the animal with their walking sticks. The out-thrust quills acted like a cushion and absorbed most of the blows. It must have taken a hundred whacks to finally knock out the porcupine. Mark flipped the body over with the tip of his stick. Both boys were exhausted by their efforts and sat down for a moment to recover.

"How will we cook him?" John asked.

"Barbecue him," Mark said. "Put chunks of meat on sticks and hold them over the fire until they're cooked."

Mark cleaned and skinned the animal, although taking off the fur was not an easy task with all those quills. The guts and skin he kicked under a nearby bush, then he hoisted the carcass. "A couple of pounds of meat there."

"Let's stop for the night and make a fire and cook supper."

"I'm ready," Mark agreed.

"My feet are killing me," John said. His feet bore several blisters that had rubbed raw and were bleeding. Mark's shoes were so light that the soles of both had almost worn through. In fact, one loose sole flapped every time he took a step. Not only was it troublesome to walk in, but it meant that foot was freezing all the time.

John found a protective bluff on one side of the stream. The ground beneath the bluff was lined with smooth polished stones and he made a semi-circle of larger stones to form a backstop for the fire. He had learned that stones stored the heat from the fire and then released it slowly throughout the night.

Mark began to cut the porcupine into little pieces. John went to the creek and found a young maple, from the trunk of which he cut half a dozen thin branches. He brought the sticks back to the fire and the boys used them as skewers to cook the porcupine meat. The pieces of meat tended to char on the outside and still be raw in the middle but they soon learned to cut the pieces small enough so that they cooked all the way through.

Gingerly John plucked a piece of cooked meat off the end of his stick and sat it on a rock to cool. "Shoot, man, I never thought food could taste so good."

"It's delicious, isn't it?" Mark agreed. "You know, if you would have told me a month ago that I'd look forward to eating porcupine meat, I'd have said you were crazy."

"That animal came just in time, too."

"You mean because we finished the last of our candies this morning?"

"Yeah." John withdrew his stick, slid a piece of meat off the sharpened point onto a rock, picked up the piece he had earlier left to cool, and popped it into his mouth. Then he stuck a new piece of raw meat on the stick and held it to the fire.

They kept about a quarter of the meat for next morning's breakfast. Mark wrapped it in some large cabbage-like leaves he found growing nearby and put the package away in the knapsack.

Following their meal, they took off their footgear and washed their feet with a wet rag that was actually a sleeve lining from Mark's jacket. Both boys now sat on the ground and Mark lifted John's feet and placed them in his lap. Gently he washed the dirt and dried blood away from the raw sores on the toes and heel.

"You know, old buddy, you sure got ugly feet," he said.

"What do you mean, ugly?" John was indignant. "Those are gorgeous feet."

"You got ugly feet is what you got," Mark insisted. "If I had feet like those I'd put them in a museum and charge admission—only two bits to see the world's ugliest feet."

"You could charge fifty cents and show them the world's baddest mouth while you're at it," John responded.

Mark grunted and lowered John's feet to the ground. He went over to the creek to wash out the rag. While he was at it, he washed out John's stockings. The water was freezing cold but he forced himself to thoroughly scrub stockings and rag before he returned to the fire. Once more he bathed his friend's feet while John held his stockings out on the end of a stick to dry in front of the fire.

"Look," Mark said, "would it do any good if I took

off my tee shirt and ripped it up to make bandages for your feet?''

"No. Those sores are gonna rub no matter what I do. Anyway, with bandages on, I couldn't get back into the shoes.''

"Yeah, well, I wish there was something we could do to make it easier for you.''

"They'll heal some tonight while I'm off my feet. I can put up with it. I'll have to. How about that open shoe of yours?''

"It's still in one piece,'' Mark said. "I'll just have to flap along on it. There's nothing else I can do.''

"Anyway, I feel a lot better after that feed.''

"Yeah. Surprising the difference it makes. I didn't even know I was hungry until I bit into that first chunk of meat.''

"I know what you mean.'' John threw another branch on to the fire. "You know, Mark, you're all right. You're a good dude, man—like you're for real.''

"So what makes you suddenly say I'm real?''

"Well, because you haven't tried to put me down, or act like you know it all. You haven't once complained that I'm holding us back because of my feet.''

"You're not holding us back,'' Mark argued.

"Yes, I am. You know we could go faster if it wasn't for me limping all the time.''

"Okay, maybe that's true, but it's going to take both of us to make it out. I mean if I got hurt, you'd help me, right?''

"Right on, brother.''

But there was something mocking in John's tone that Mark noticed. He shrugged it off, however, then reluctantly got to his feet. "I'm going to get more wood."

"You want some help?"

"Naw, you rest your feet. I'll manage."

"A lot of the bottom branches on those evergreens are dead and will snap right off," John said.

"Yeah, okay."

It took Mark almost an hour to gather enough wood to last through the night but finally he had a huge bundle of dead branches stacked up beside the fire. It soon grew dark and the boys sat in front of the flickering flames, their one blanket draped around their shoulders.

John shivered, then spread his hands to the fire. "Mark?"

"Yeah," Mark answered sleepily.

"Let's go on with that trip."

"Okay. Where did we leave off?"

"Outside of London. Remember we rode the bus to the end of the line and then got off?"

"Okay. Now two trucks have passed us without stopping but here comes a big Rolls Royce just purring along and guess what?"

"He's slowing down for us?"

"Dream on. He just speeded up again. But here's a sort of English pick-up stopping for us and the guy tells us to hop in the back."

"Is the truck empty?"

"Yeah, all it's got is some shovels and rakes. The guy is a gardener or something."

"Where's he taking us?"

"To a village called Farnham. He lets us out on the town square and I ask him if there's any place around we can buy a couple of bicycles and he says there's a bicycle store on High Street."

"Hey, how come we didn't buy our bicycles in London?" John asked.

"Because we didn't like all that heavy traffic, remember? We figured it would be better to get out of the city before we started to cycle."

"Oh yeah, that's right."

"Anyway, we find the bicycle store."

"Okay."

"And the guy is nice and all but he tries to sell us new bikes. I keep telling him we want second-hand bikes and finally he shows us these two old bikes. Actually, they're not bad looking. They got three speeds and all but there's one little problem."

"Too expensive?"

"No, he only wants eight pounds apiece."

"So what's the problem then?"

"One of them is a girl's bike."

"No sweat—we'll flip a coin."

"Okay, I got one of those English tuppeny pieces. You call."

"Heads," John called.

"Here we go. Heads it is. I guess I get the girl's bike. Okay, we've paid him. Oh, and I buy one of those little repair kits in case we get a flat. Now we wheel the bicycles out of the shop and onto the street and away we go. Hey, this is great.''

''Wait a minute. What color's my bike?''

''Black,'' Mark answered.

''That figgers.''

''Now we're heading down High Street. We just passed a butcher shop and now a bakery. Ummm, that smell.''

''Yeah.'' John closed his eyes. ''Newly baked bread.''

''And new-mown hay,'' Mark added.

''And purple fruited plains.''

''Okay,'' said Mark. ''Now here's a kid crossing in front of me and I ring the bell at him.''

''So do I. By the way, where are we going?''

''Just hacking around. You hungry yet?''

''I guess I could eat a sandwich.''

''Okay, we'll look for a tea shop.''

''Oh hey, wow, a tea shop, cool, man.''

The fire burned low as the two boys continued with their journey. Finally John curled up and went to sleep, while Mark kept watch on the fire. At midnight Mark woke John and they changed places, Mark now curled up in the blanket while John kept the fire going.

Finally a gray light began to filter through the treetops and slowly bring things into focus. There were no branches left and the fire had burned down to a low mound of ashes. Mark mumbled something in his sleep and John was about to waken him when he heard a very faint, faraway noise. He lifted his head and strained as hard as he could. The noise came once more. The sound was barely audible but it had the unmistakable dying moan of a train whistle.

Eagerly John reached forward to shake Mark awake.

13

Old Mr. Lusty was writing in his journal. For the past few days now, it had become more and more difficult to write. After half a dozen words his fingers would tire so that he would have to stop for a minute or so before going on to the next sentence. He read over what he had written so far for that day. "Desmond very sick, running high fever. I too lots weaker. Marshal lies on floor all day. Not able to hunt. When he tries to walk, his hip gives out. Annie still goes for water. We are losing hope. Mark and John now our only chance."

Mr. Lusty put the legal pad back in the briefcase. He looked over at Desmond who was curled up in a ball on the floor. Every half hour or so Desmond would break into a fit of uncontrollable shivering. Each time he did so, Annie would hold him until the shivering passed, then bathe his sweating brow with a moistened piece of cloth. For a while Desmond would be all right, then he would begin to shiver again and apologize. "I'm sorry," he would say, over and over again. "I'm sorry."

It was during one of these seizures that he suddenly sat up and cried out, "Quick! Pile on the branches!"

For a moment Annie thought his mind was wandering. Then she too caught the sound of the airplane engine. On her knees now, she shoveled green branches into the fireplace with her hands until a thick cloud of white smoke was rolling up the chimney.

Then she got to her feet and snatched the water bowl from the table. Hurrying outside, she emptied the water and tried to flash a signal up at the sky. The heavy overcast of the night before had given way to odd scattered clouds scudding swiftly by.

The plane sounded near, closer than any plane had ever come before. But no matter how she searched the sky, Annie could not see the aircraft anywhere. All the while she kept stumbling from one sunny spot to another, trying to catch the rays of sun and redirect them skyward with her bowl. All the while the sound of the airplane engine grew fainter and fainter until finally it died away and the sky was one vast pitiless silence.

She stared at the ridge line of a nearby mountain, beyond which the plane had last been heard. Perhaps it would come back. Perhaps . . .

She heard a noise and turned around. Mr. Lusty had come out of the cabin and was now slowly, painfully, with the aid of a stick he had picked up somewhere, making his way toward her. She felt sorry for him, for his thin pipestem legs and arms, his parchment-like skin, his bent shoulders, and the black thrust-up veins on each side of his forehead. Then she realized that of them all, he had complained the least. In fact she couldn't recall his ever having complained about anything since the crash.

"Why couldn't the pilot have seen our smoke?" she asked. "There was plenty of it."

Mr. Lusty stopped and leaned on his stick. "Maybe he did."

"But wouldn't he fly down over the cabin if he saw the smoke? Wouldn't he let us know that he had found us?"

"He would if he were looking for us," Lusty said. "But he might assume that we're just some trappers, or campers."

"But it sounded like he was circling around up there, looking for something," Annie said.

"Well, yes it did, but that could mean anything. Maybe it's a wildlife patrol plane out looking for bands of deer or elk."

"Well, if the marshal's right, they're looking in the wrong place," Annie said. Then suddenly the complaints and fear spilled out of her, along with a burst of tears. "And we need more firewood, and more green branches to make smoke with, and I'm the only one who can do it all and I'm too tired, and too hungry and too lonely and too frightened. . . ."

Mr. Lusty took the water bowl out of her hands.

"There, there now. Don't despair, Annie. I'll get the water," he said. "It'll take me a little while but I'll manage it. You go now and gather an armful of firewood. The green branches we can leave until later in the day, or even tomorrow."

"I'm sorry," Annie said. "I know I should be better. I just can't help myself. What's going to happen to us, Mr. Lusty?"

"We're going to be rescued," he said. "I feel it. In fact help is probably on the way to us right now."

"Do you think so?"

"I firmly believe it."

Annie managed a smile. "All right, I'll get some wood." She walked off into the trees.

Mr. Lusty made his way to the stream. He had a tendency now to get lightheaded when he bent down, but he overcame his fear and his dizziness and managed to fill the bowl with water. Then, his walking stick thrust under one arm, he carefully carried the bowl in his cupped hands back to the cabin.

Ten minutes later Annie returned with an armful of branches. She dumped the branches in one corner and went over to Desmond. He stirred, then sat up. His eyes were unnaturally bright and his face was flushed. "Could I have some water?"

Annie brought him a cup of water from the bowl. Desmond gulped it down. "I've gotta go outside," he said.

"Yes. Do you need help?" Annie asked.

Desmond shakily got to his feet. "I'm okay." Somehow he made it to the door. He seemed to spend a long time outside and Annie was about to go looking for him when the cabin door opened and Desmond lurched back in. Silently he went to the fire, sat down on the floor, then stretched out, drawing a blanket up over him.

By now the passage of the plane had thrown everyone into a gloomy, pessimistic mood. In the beginning they had thought that if a plane came anywhere near them, they could expect to be seen and eventually rescued. But now they had heard, and even seen, at least half a dozen planes. Yet there was no sign that any of the pilots had spotted either the cabin or the wreckage.

"I never thought pilots were so stupid," the marshal said.

No one contradicted him.

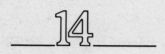

14

"I still say that was a train whistle I heard yesterday morning," John insisted.

"I hope you're right," Mark said. "If we run across railroad tracks we'll be okay. We can build a fire beside them and wait for the first train that comes along."

"But what else could it be?" John demanded.

"I don't know. Maybe a whistle from a sawmill, or a logging camp, or even a trick of the wind."

The boys were floundering around on the side of the creek. Since morning they had been battling heavy underbrush. Several times they had moved out wide on both sides of the water, looking for clear ground, but each time they had had to return because the underbrush showed no signs of thinning out.

Hour after hour they threaded their way through the wiry branches and thorny vines of the undergrowth. John's face hurt all the time now. His broken tooth caused him almost constant pain. In addition, he had been badly scratched by a briar branch that had whipped back and dragged across one cheek, leaving an irregular line of ruby red scabs on his face.

Mark's right shoe had almost disintegrated. He had to be extra careful where he placed his foot each time. If a vine or creeper caught between the sole and the upper, it could rip the bottom completely off his shoe. And if that happened he would have to slog on in his stocking feet.

"Ah shoot, I'm bushed," John called out. "Let's rest for a minute."

Mark heaved a big sigh and turned around. He waited for John to catch up.

"You know what I keep thinking?" John asked.

"What?"

"I keep thinking the guys back at the cabin have already been rescued."

"Yeah, but they would have told somebody about us, and an airplane would be out, trying to pick up our trail."

"Heck, in this underbrush no pilot would ever spot us."

"Fine, but so far we haven't heard any low-flying planes."

"Yeah, I know," John said glumly. He sat down on a fallen log. "Planes, planes, planes," he sighed. "We owe all this to planes and a hijacker!"

"Yep, but he got his."

"Right. But I still can't help wondering about that guy. 'Lawn mower's on the fritz.' And those numbers, 'ten-four.' You suppose he was trying to tell us something?''

"Who knows, Sherlock Holmes?" Mark laughed.

"Okay, okay, but if somebody said 'ten-four' and asked you to guess what it meant, what would you say?" John asked.

"I don't know," Mark said. "It could be some sort of code. It could be a date in history. Charlemagne was crowned emperor in ten-four or was it nine, ninety nine? Mathematically it could be part of a series, the set before being 'nine-three' and the set after 'eleven-five.' Or it could be part of a series where the larger number is always two and a half times the smaller number as in 'fifteen six' or 'twenty-five ten.' "

John gave a sigh. "Remind me never to ask you a simple question."

"So what's the point?"

"Cops use that number, at least they do on TV shows. When they're using their radios and want to sign off, they say 'ten-four,' and that's what the hijacker said."

"Okay. So?"

"Weird thing for a bank robber to say, isn't it?" John asked.

"You still worrying about that? He was probably brought to the airport in a patrol car. Maybe he picked it up from the police car radio."

"Okay, but it still bothers me." John stood up and stretched. "Well, let's get movin'."

In mid-afternoon they called another halt. John had

climbed the last lookout tree early in the morning, so it was Mark's turn to go aloft and look around.

Mark sat down and took off his loose shoe. Using half a shoelace he bound up the flopping sole to the rest of the shoe. He put the shoe back on and looked around for a tree that would give good visibility and also be easy to climb. He finally selected a pine with a fair spread of branches and began to ascend. Soon he was within fifteen feet of the crown.

Standing on a branch and holding the trunk with one hand, Mark called down, "Wow, there's really a view from up here!"

John moved away from the tree a good twenty yards so he could see Mark up near the top. "See any smoke?"

"No, but I think I see some railway tracks, or maybe even a road."

"No kidding!"

"Yeah, there's a sort of straight line through the trees. It runs across the side of a hill about three miles ahead of us."

"That close?"

"Maybe a little more, maybe four or five miles."

"Can we reach it before dark?"

"I think so. We're gonna have to leave the stream though and then go uphill for a mile or so. Tell you one thing, that cut is too straight to be natural—it has to be man-made."

"That's great!" John said. "Okay, come on down, but be careful."

"Right."

Mark started down. He wrapped his legs around the trunk, caught a branch with his hand, and slid down four or five feet. Then he changed position. His right foot now resting on a broken-off stub of a branch, he dropped the left foot as far as he could, reaching with his toes for a lower branch. At that moment the branch end bearing the weight of his right foot cracked sharply and Mark's heart skipped a beat. To his horror he found himself growing dizzy and losing consciousness. "Hang on," he scolded himself, only to discover that his body refused to respond to his commands. Then he knew, with an awful finality, that he was going to fall all the way.

John was horrified as he watched Mark come plummeting down through the tree. "Grab on!" he shouted and broke into a run. His friend's body turned a slow pinwheel. Some branches sheared off when Mark hit them, while others bent and threw his body off to one side.

Mark broke through the last, lowest skirt of branches and hit the ground just as John got there. For a moment it looked as though Mark had landed on his feet but then he crumpled and fell to his knees.

John bent down and rolled Mark over on to his back. Mark's eyes were rolled back and John was close to panic. "Wake up!" he yelled. "Come on, come on, man, wake up. Let's go, Mark, you gotta wake up!"

Mark's eyes opened. For a moment they stared blankly ahead, registering nothing.

— 114

"You okay?"

The eyes came into focus and picked out the worried face of John looming above. "Yeah, I'm okay. No, I'm not. My foot." Mark closed his eyes, stretched out one leg and gave a long low moan of pain. His face went ashen white and beads of sweat formed on his forehead and upper lip.

"What is it? What's wrong?"

"My foot. I think it's broken. The ankle hurts like crazy."

"Oh God," John groaned. "Can you stand up on your good leg?"

"I'll try."

John lifted Mark to his feet, then held him upright. Mark stood on his good leg. His right leg was slightly bent at the knee, the toe of his shoe barely touching the ground.

"Can you put any weight on that leg?"

Mark shook his head. "No way. I'll only pass out from the pain."

"Okay, now take it easy. Lean your weight on me." John guided Mark over to a fallen log, then made him sit on the ground, using the trunk of the dead tree as a support for his back.

"Stretch out both legs," John said. Working as gently as he could, he removed Mark's shoe and stocking, then whistled when he saw the ankle. It was as though Mark were wearing a small pink balloon around his foot. The swelling had puffed up the skin and left it tight as a drum.

"You got a bad sprain there, old buddy," John said.

"Sprain? It feels more like it's broken."

"Well, whatever it is, it sure'n hell don't look very pretty. The question is, what should we do about it? We could make a bandage of some kind, but I'm not sure that's the best thing. I mean I'm no doctor."

"We're going to have to wait until the swelling goes down before we think about bandages," Mark agreed.

"Darn it all, I told you to be careful up there."

"I was. But I just got faint and weak all of a sudden on my way down. My body had no strength, I just couldn't hold on to anything."

John crouched so that he was facing Mark. "So what do we do now? Just leave it the way it is?"

"Maybe try and get the sock back on. Could we light a fire and stop for the night?"

"I don't know," John said. "If I cut a crutch of some kind, and you leaned your arm on my shoulder, do you think you could hobble along for a while? Because if there's a road down there, and help, then I think we should keep moving as long as we can."

John picked up the discarded shoe and tucked it in the knapsack. "No point in even trying to get this back on."

"Okay, but how about my sock?"

Working as slowly and delicately as he could, John managed to get the sock back on to Mark's foot without causing his friend too much pain. Then he left Mark and went ranging out into the woods, looking for a suitable branch. He finally found a hefty Y-shaped sapling that looked as though it would do the job. Patiently he chis-eled through it with Mark's pocketknife. He brought the staff back, assisted Mark to his feet, and urged him to try out the home-made crutch. Mark placed the Y end under his right armpit and swung his left foot for-ward.

"How does it feel?" John asked.

"Fine. It might be a little long, but I'll manage."

"Better a little long," John said. "The bottom will soon wear down." John then made a sweeping bow, crooked his right arm and said, "Well, madame, shall we proceed?"

Mark forced a grin and hobbled forward. Their prog-ress was slower than ever and to add to their troubles, the light began to fail early as clouds, building up all day, started to release their burden of rain.

"I don't know what's worse, the snow or the rain," John complained.

"Yeah, I know what you mean. The rain gets you wet all over, while the snow keeps your feet frozen."

"Well, at least the rain means that it has warmed up some."

"Yeah. Don't you think we ought to stop soon? It's getting dark and I don't know how much longer I can keep this up."

"Yeah, soon," John promised. "Look, you said the stream made a sharp left turn when we hit the bottom of a draw, and that to reach what you thought was a road, we had to leave the stream and go uphill for a mile or so?"

117 __

"That's right. I think this stream runs into another one at the bottom of the draw, like a T."

"Yeah, well, I've been thinking. It would be nice if we could reach the bottom of this hill tonight. Then in the morning I could hike up and see what the road or trail looks like. If it looked good, then I could come back for you. But if not, we could just continue to follow the creek."

"Okay," Mark agreed. "Let's shove on then!"

But dark found them still short of the canyon bottom. Despite Mark's tiredness and pain, John insisted on moving ahead. For one thing they had broken out of the underbrush and were now cautiously feeling their way down an open grassy hillside that was dotted here and there with solitary pines. John was sure that they were close to the bottom and kept urging Mark to bear up.

The downhill slope made it even more difficult for Mark to keep his balance. In addition to everything else, the rain had melted the top quarter inch of frozen soil and left the surface of the hill very slippery. Mark felt the ground give out from under his crutch as a clump of grass tore loose from the hill and slid away beneath the pressure of his staff. He lost his balance, flung out his arms, and fell backwards, letting out a shout.

John turned around. It was obvious that Mark was close to the limit of his endurance. Yet John was sure that they could reach the bottom of the hill with just another few minutes of walking. He went back and helped Mark to his feet. As the latter placed the crutch under his armpit, his foot kicked a rock loose and it bounded away. The stone bounced once on the frozen ground and was then swallowed up by the night. Something about the silence that followed the stone's fall, something about the dead quality of the sound of their voices, something about the hint of echoes around them, caused John to hold up his hand and stop Mark. John lifted a stone from the ground and lobbed it out in front of him. There was no sound at all. He gave a shiver and decided that perhaps it was time to stop for the night.

He remembered seeing a pair of large evergreens just off to their left and said, "Come on, there's some shelter over here." He lifted Mark's arm, placed it around his shoulders, and helped him negotiate the tricky, half-frozen ground. They reached two huge pines that seemed to grow up out of a single root. The V space between the trees was filled with dead leaves and twigs. John scooped away at this debris until he had hollowed out a fair-sized depression.

"I think we better skip a fire tonight," he said. "I'm not about to go rooting around in the dark looking for wood."

"No. Anyway, you're not going to find any dry wood," Mark agreed.

"I think we'd better just curl up here and try to sleep. Is there anything I can do for that ankle?" John helped Mark sit down and arrange himself. Mark kept the bad leg sticking straight out. John joined his friend and for warmth both boys sat as close as possible to each other, a single blanket covering their bodies.

After half an hour of silence, Mark called softly, "John?"

"Yeah?"

"I can't sleep."

"Me neither."

"My ankle throbs like a giant toothache."

"Yeah, and there's water dripping down my neck from somewhere."

"John?"

"Yeah?"

"I don't think we're gonna make it. In the morning I'm not going to be able to move this foot at all. I can tell."

"We'll make it, don't worry. Anyway, you can't cop out on me now. If I have to, I'll carry you."

"I think it would be better if you went on alone in the morning. I'm only going to slow things to a crawl. Like you could always come back for me, when you reach somebody."

"Look, we'll talk about it in the morning, okay? Now let's try and get some sleep."

"Okay."

They tried to arrange their bodies and the blanket so as to make themselves as comfortable as possible. For another half an hour all was quiet. Then John's voice broke the stillness.

"Mark?"

"Yeah?"

"You sleeping?"

— 120

"No."

"You want to go on with our bicycle tour? You don't have to, like it's up to you. I just thought maybe it would help pass the time, maybe make us sleepy."

"Where'd we stop the last time?" Mark asked.

"We were looking for a place to stay. We were in Cornwall and it was too far to the next youth hostel so we were looking for a cheap place to stay."

"Oh yeah, now I remember. We were wheeling along this narrow English road. There are these tall hedges on each side of the road. There are lovely green fields all around, everywhere we look, and once in a while we see a thatched cottage. Anyway, we decide to stop, so we lean our bicycles against the hedge and we sit down beside the road and we just lie back on the grass and enjoy the afternoon sun while we think about getting something to eat and a place to stay for the night."

"What time is it?"

"You mean here or in England?"

"England."

"Oh, it's about four o'clock. Anyway, we're just sitting there taking it easy, when a cow suddenly appears, running down the middle of the road. We're very cool about this so we just sit there and watch the animal. Then an old man shows up, running along waving a stick, and he shouts at us, 'Head her off like a good chap!' So we stand up and the cow comes to a stop and snorts at us a couple of times, only by now the farmer has come up and tied a rope around her neck."

"So the farmer thanks us," John said.

"Right. And we get into a conversation with him and the next thing he's inviting us home to his house."

"I hope he's going to offer us something to eat," John said.

"Don't worry, I'm coming to that," Mark promised.

And while they shivered in the cold, and the rain poured down, Mark described a lunch that included Stilton cheese and Somerset cider, steak and kidney pie, Devon clotted cream over fresh strawberries, and mug after mug of steaming tea.

15

The lines of a country and western song he had once heard on a car radio kept running through Desmond's head. They described almost exactly how he felt. "His belly fell down and his back caved in." That was how he felt all right, like his belly had shriveled away to almost nothing and his back had caved in. And if that weren't enough, his lungs ached all the time and his head felt like a big empty box.

Desmond opened his eyes and looked across at Marshal O'Connor who was laying out the cards for one of his endless games of Patience. "How many rounds do you have for that gun of yours?" he asked.

"Six," the marshal said.

"Don't you think you ought to try and shoot one of those blue jays Annie keeps seeing? And this time I'm not kidding."

"I saw them again this morning," Annie said.

"I thought we were going to save the bullets for bigger game," the marshal argued.

"In the meantime we're starving," Desmond pointed out.

O'Connor patted his pocket. "It's not going to be easy to hit a blue jay with a thirty-eight. And even if I should hit one, there isn't going to be much left. These slugs do an awful lot of damage."

Annie jumped into the argument. "Well, I think you ought to try. You haven't seen any deer, and there's only been that one rabbit, so there's no sense in saving your ammunition. Anyway you hardly ever go outside any more, so how are you going to shoot anything?"

"She's right, you know," Mr. Lusty said.

"Right or wrong I'm not going to throw these bullets away on a blue jay. You kids have no idea how hard it is to hit a bird with a handgun like a thirty-eight."

"Why don't we heat up another run of rabbit soup?" Mr. Lusty said. Anytime an argument broke out, the old man acted as peacemaker. He had saved half a paper cup of splintered bones that remained from their first meal and used them to boil up succeeding rounds of rabbit soup. The amount of nourishment left on the bones was practically nothing, but it was enough to give the hot water a very faint soupy taste and the barest hint of a pale gray color. And although everyone agreed that the soup was practically indistinguishable from hot water, no one passed up his share.

Sitting on one side of the fire, Annie sipped the soup

and thought about her hunger. She thought of all the times she had refused to eat breakfast, of all the second helpings she had waved away, of all the school lunches she had passed up. She would be thankful now for one of those pasty cheese sandwiches they gave you in the cafeteria. Let's face it, she would even be happy to sort through the garbage and pick out the crusts thrown away by the other kids.

The soup failed to cheer anyone up and an apathetic silence fell on the four people. These hopeless silences now lasted longer and longer. In the beginning they used to sing songs to pass the time and to keep up their spirits, but after a while they recognized that singing, and even talking, burned up calories they could not afford to lose. So they just sat there, half asleep most of the time, stirring themselves only to put more wood on the fire, or to go to the creek for water, or to go outside to the bathroom.

It was during one of these long silences that Desmond opened his eyes, thought he saw something, and said, "Sssh, what's that?"

"What's what?" Annie whispered back.

"In the corner."

"Where? Oh!"

In the far corner of the cabin, a squirrel sat up on his hind legs, his thick bushy tail curving up and along his back.

"It's a rat," Annie whispered.

"No, no, it's a squirrel," Desmond said. "Ssssh, I'm going to kill it." He reached out with his hand and

125 —

picked up a branch that they used to poke at the fire. Moving as slowly as possible, he got up on the balls of his feet and into a crouch. Slowly he advanced on the corner, moving in a sort of duck waddle. He did not dare to stand upright, fearing that the move would scare the squirrel back into hiding.

The small gray statue stood still in the corner, only the tail moving now and again in quick sharp twitches and ripples.

"Careful," Annie whispered. She was surprised at the sudden show of strength from Desmond. In his eagerness to kill the animal, he seemed to have forgotten his sickness, his weakness, his pain. His face tight with concentration, he waddled another step closer, the stick held ready in his right hand. He waited a long moment, hoping to lull the animal into a sense of security. Then cautiously he moved another step closer.

The squirrel dropped to all fours and Desmond sprang, bringing his club down on the exact spot where the animal had been sitting. There was a flash of gray and Desmond swung again. Then he went berserk, screaming and beating the floor and walls in the corner. The stick snapped in two and Desmond whirled and threw the broken half across the cabin. It bounced off the door and landed at Annie's feet.

"It's all your fault," Desmond screamed at the marshal. "Why didn't you shoot it? Why are you so stupid, sitting there day after day! What does an animal have to do before you shoot it, go down on its knees and beg?"

"I never saw it until you were practically on top of it,

and then I might have hit you," the marshal reasoned.

"Take it easy, Desmond, it's not the marshal's fault," Mr. Lusty said. "I didn't see the animal either."

By now Desmond had sunk to the floor, his back against a wall, and was openly crying. "Oh God, I'm sorry, everybody," he cried out between sobs. "I'm sorry. I'm sorry."

"It's not your fault, Desmond" Annie tried to comfort him.

"I'm sorry. I'm sorry about the sandwich," Desmond said.

"The sandwich?" Annie repeated.

"Yes, I'm sorry."

Annie shook her head, unable to make any sense out of Desmond's apology.

"He must think he ate the sandwich we gave to John and Mark," O'Connor said.

"No," Desmond said. "Not that one, the other one."

"Other one? There was only *one* sandwich," Annie said.

"I'm afraid he's delirious," Mr. Lusty said.

Desmond gave a bitter laugh. "Oh what's the use? We've had it, we're done for. We're all going to die in this miserable hole."

"Oh shut up, Desmond," Annie said, in a sudden flare of temper.

Desmond turned away into a corner and began to cough. The coughs turned into dry hacking heaves as sweat thickly beaded his forehead.

"Desmond? Are you all right?" Annie asked, feeling bad for snapping at him.

Desmond shook his head. He was looking down at a spreading stain on the floor. Something was very wrong with him, he was throwing up blood.

16

"Oh boy," John said softly, "were we lucky!"

He was sitting up, looking down the slope. There, not twenty feet below him, the hill stopped abruptly at a cliff edge. John found a small stone and lobbed it out into space. Seconds later he heard a clink as the stone hit another stone at the bottom of the cliff.

"What's wrong?" Mark sat up.

John advanced to the edge of the precipice. It was a sheer drop of fifty feet to the bottom of the canyon. He looked across at the opposite hillside but there was no sign of any road or railroad line. Still, all those trees did not make it easy to spot anything.

Mark was looking at his swollen foot. He got the stocking off and touched the proud red flesh around the ankle. His forefinger left a white spot that did not turn pink again for a good half minute.

"At least it doesn't look any worse than it did last night," John said. "Does it still hurt as bad?"

"Yeah, I think it's broken."

"Just make sure to keep your weight off it."

"Don't worry, I'm not about to stand on it."

"You see the cliff there?" John pointed. "Were we lucky we stopped when we did last night. Another few feet and one of us would have fallen over."

"Yeah. The thing is, how are we going to reach the bottom?" Mark asked.

"Be right back." John walked away, following the contour of the hill. A few minutes later he returned. "It's what I figured. A bit further on the whole side of the hill sluffs off in a sort of rock slide. It's fairly steep but I think we'll manage."

With some difficulty Mark got to his feet. John rolled up the blanket and stuffed it into his pack. "Okay, I'll go first," he said. "I'll try and pick out the easiest way and you just follow me, okay?"

Mark nodded.

"Shout if I'm going too fast for you, or if you want to stop for any reason," John advised.

"Don't worry, I will." Mark planted the end of his crutch on the grass and swung himself forward.

Half an hour later the cliff turned into a steep slope of loose rocks and pebbles. Both boys halted and examined the rock slide for a moment. John stepped out on the gravel and his feet sent a wave of small stones building up below him. He could maneuver on the slope without too much trouble, but Mark would never be able to make it down on his own. He turned to face his friend and was momentarily shocked at Mark's appearance. His eyes had a dead look, the skin drawn tight over the cheekbones, and his whole head was beginning to take on a skull-like appearance.

"The leg still hurts, huh?"

Mark grimaced and closed his eyes. "Yeah."

"You didn't get much sleep either last night?"

"No."

"Well, look, we gotta figure out some way of getting you down this slope. Then I'll build a fire at the bottom and you can rest, dry out your clothes, and maybe even catch a nap." It had stopped raining during the night, but not before their clothes had been thoroughly soaked.

"How? I'll never make it down with this leg."

"I'm going to have to carry you down. It's the only way. Put your arms around my neck and hang on."

John sat down on the gravel, his back to Mark. "Okay, hop on."

Mark put his arms around John's neck, resting most of his weight on his friend's back. John took Mark's crutch in one hand to use as a staff, then pushed himself erect. For a moment he swayed perilously. Then he steadied himself and took a step forward. His foot sank to the ankle in the loose stones but the slope held and he took another cautious step forward.

Four times they had to stop for a rest before they made it to the bottom of the rubble slope. Here John left

Mark with his back against a tree while he climbed back up the slope to retrieve his coat and knapsack. When he came back, he got Mark to his feet and they moved to a spot right beside the stream. Once again Mark sat down and John tried to get a fire going. He found an old pine stump and managed to stab and dig out a handful of pitch-laden chips. Then he followed the stream downhill until he found a log jam of water-borne wood. He selected an armload of the driest branches and brought them back to where Mark was sitting. With the help of the pine chips and some dry paper from inside his shirt, he was able to get a decent fire going. Then he left Mark drying his clothes at the flames while he went out to scavenge more firewood.

Altogether he carried eight armloads of branches back to the fire and spread them out in such a way that the heat from the flames would help dry out the wood. Finally he sat down beside Mark and began to dry his own clothes. He got his shoes off, then held his stockings up to the heat. Mark was leaning forward, his jacket held up. Wisps of steam rose from the wet fabric.

"I figure we got enough wood there for at least twenty-four hours," John said.

"Yeah. What do we do now?" Mark turned his jacket around.

"What do we do?" John repeated. "Here's what we do. I'm going across that stream and up that hill and look for that road or whatever it was you saw yesterday, right?"

"Right."

John checked Mark's watch. "Okay, it's a quarter to ten. Say I dry out and try to grab some sleep until 12:30. And say it gets dark about 6:30. That leaves me six hours. Say I go up that hill and straight on for three hours. Even if I don't run across something, I've still got three hours to make it back before dark."

"You could probably hike for three and a half hours and leave yourself two and a half hours to return because you'll have it downhill most of the way coming back."

"Okay, I'll do that," John agreed. "But right now I'm gonna try and grab some rest. Will you wake me at 12:30?"

"Sure."

John curled up as close as he could to the flames. But sleep did not come easy. For one thing he was wet to the skin. And for another thing he kept thinking back on the plane crash. There was still something bothering him. What was it? Two men in the aisle by the john, talking to the stewardess. Had to be the hijacker and Talmage. Then later the hijacker came back, just before the crash. The marshal had been sitting in the back of the plane. Yet the marshal had not seen the hijacker, when he came rushing back. If he had, he would have said something or done something.

John groaned and turned over. Before the crash, two men going up the aisle. A man's hand on the seat back in front of him. A red mark around the wrist? Why? Earlier he had turned around and looked at the three men sitting in the back of the plane. He had not known then who they were. It was annoying, something there but he could not put his finger on it.

The next thing Mark was shaking him awake. "C'mon John, it's half past twelve."

"Wow, did I sleep all that time?" He sat up and rubbed his eyes.

"Yeah, but I don't know how good a sleep it was. You kept moaning and groaning and twitching."

John shivered and spread his hands to the fire. "It's cold. I'm freezing."

"Well get yourself good and warm before you take off."

Minutes later John got to his feet and stretched. "Okay, look for me to come back around dark. If I'm not back before dark it will mean that I've reached somebody and help is on the way."

"Okay," Mark said doubtfully. "Here, take my watch."

"Now look, man, don't panic." John strapped on the watch. He could tell that Mark was upset at being left all alone. "No matter what happens, I won't abandon you."

"Just don't do something stupid like I did and hurt yourself."

"Don't worry, I'll be careful. Now, just in case I don't make it back before dark, you should have enough wood for the rest of the night. Just keep the fire small and try to make it last. And you got plenty of water right there in the creek."

"Okay. Do you still have matches in case you want to light a fire?"

"Yeah, I got matches here somewhere, but I don't think I'll need them."

"Where are they? Let me see them."

"They're in my shirt somewhere," John said, as his hands went rummaging through his pockets.

"Let me see them," Mark insisted.

John finally found the matches and showed them to Mark.

"Okay, now make sure you put them back in an inside pocket where they won't get damp."

"Okay, mother." John squatted down and put one hand on Mark's shoulder. "Now look, old buddy, don't get to worrying. If I'm not back before dark, then it means I've found help and we're waiting until daylight to come back for you."

"Okay. I won't start wringing my hands and weeping and wailing until tomorrow night at least." Mark managed a smile.

"Good." John stood up and walked away a few paces.

"Hey?" Mark called after his friend.

"Yeah?"

"Don't forget, we got a trip to make this summer."

"Trip? Oh, you mean England?"

"I certainly do."

"Okay man, I won't forget," John said.

"But hey, I really mean it," Mark insisted.

135 —

"You mean the two of us buy bicycles and all, and cycle around England together?"

"Sure. We got to see if the real trip lives up to our imaginary one. Come on, it will be fun to hack around together in England and see what the country is like."

"You know what it's like, you been there before," John pointed out.

"Me?" Mark said in surprise. "I've never set foot in England in my life."

"You said you were in Europe before."

"Yeah, but not in England."

"You mean all that stuff you been feeding me is a line of bull?"

Mark grinned. "Not exactly. Some of it I got from English movies, and some of it from reading books about England, and some of it I made up."

"Well, you sure had me conned."

"So how about it?" Mark asked.

John walked back and stuck out his hand. "Shake. You got yourself a deal."

"Great!"

"That is, if we both come out of this mess okay."

"We will," Mark insisted. "I got faith in you, man."

"You know, for an okay dude you're really something special," John said with a smile, then waved and stepped out. He walked along the stream until he found a jumbled mass of timber that formed a partial dam across the water. He got up on an old fallen tree and picked his way across the makeshift bridge until he reached the far side. There he stopped for a moment to examine the slope of trees above him, trying to plot an easy path through the timber and brush.

By now John no longer felt hungry. It was as though his stomach knew there was no fuel for it and had given up sending any more messages. His chief problem was that he tired very quickly and had to rest much more often than he normally would. He particularly felt it in his legs. He also got an odd dizzy spell that usually came when he tried to stand up after sitting for a while. His coordination was poor, he noticed. His hands felt like blocks of wood, as though they were half frozen, and if he wanted to take something out of his pocket, he had to fumble around a long time before getting the object free.

Wearily he dug in his toes, reached for a sapling, and pulled himself erect. After an hour of steady climbing, he sat down on the ground for a rest. Elbows on knees, head bent and resting in his hands, he drew in long shuddering breaths. After five minutes or so his breathing returned to normal. He was trying to go too fast, he realized. He would have to slow down and rest more often. He wanted to cover as much ground as he could before he had to turn back, but there was no point in knocking himself out either.

He forced himself to rest another minute or two, then stood up. What he would do was, he would pace himself; take a minute rest after every hundred steps, and a sitting down ten-minute break after every thousand steps. He moved ahead and began to count.

At three o'clock he broke out on level ground for a while. The land was still heavily wooded but was now flat and he guessed that he had reached some sort of upland plateau. It felt good not to have to walk uphill all the time. And maybe his uphill hiking was over because he would have to think soon about turning back. Whatever that road was that Mark thought he had seen, he should have reached it by now. He resumed counting: 391, 392, and at 400 he called a halt. He walked over and sat on a large round boulder, then checked the time: twelve minutes past three. He would take his ten-minute break at 500 paces instead of one thousand. At three-twenty he would start up again and walk another 500 paces. If he didn't find anything then, he would turn back.

Rested, he got to his feet and moved ahead. He was almost sure now that he wasn't going to find a road or anything like that. Mark had probably seen something else, a natural line of trees perhaps, or maybe some fault in the land.

John detoured around a thick clump of pines, then stopped and let out a grunt of surprise. Railroad tracks! He stumbled forward some twenty yards, crouched down, and patted the shiny rail. So he really had heard a train whistle the other morning! He looked to his left, then to his right. Grass grew high between the wooden sleepers and he would have said that it was an abandoned railway line except that the rails shone brightly, with no signs of rust, which meant that the trains were regularly using the tracks. In fact on one sleeper there was a gob of fresh oil that could not have been more than a few days old. The question now was, how often was the line being used? Once a day? Or once a week?

For the moment though he had better see to getting a fire lighted. He scurried around looking for some dead wood. Strangely enough, his tiredness and exhaustion completely left him as he tramped around gathering wood. What he would do was, he would stay all night and all day beside the tracks. If he stayed a full twenty-four hours, he should catch at least one train passing by. If none came by before three o'clock tomorrow afternoon, he would hike back to Mark and they would have to come up with some other plan.

It was while carrying another armload of branches over to a space he had cleared beside the tracks that John realized he was whistling! He shook his head in amazement. He hadn't whistled in so long he had almost forgotten how.

17

For the hundredth time Annie went to the window to look out at the clearing, hoping against hope to see a rescue party making their way toward the cabin. She even knew what the rescuers would be like, three great big men wearing uniforms and carrying huge packs stuffed with food and supplies. They would be in single file, linked to each other with a rope, and the leader would have a tall bicycle pennant with a triangular red flag sticking up from his pack. The flag would be jauntily dipping and waving with each step the leader took.

But there were no rescuers out there and she stared at the scene several moments before the animals registered on her brain. The five beautiful deer were so unexpected they might have been a dream. A large buck with a full spread of horns, two does, and two fawns were delicately cropping the grass. Even as she watched, a fawn went bouncing stiff-legged over to its mother. The small head pushed at the female's flank as the fawn sought milk.

"Marshal," Annie whispered. "Get your gun. There's deer outside, a whole bunch of them."

"Deer?" the marshal said. Slowly he got to his feet and fumbled the heavy revolver out of his jacket pocket.

"Ssssh, quiet, don't scare them," Mr. Lusty warned.

"Deer?" Desmond repeated, sitting up. "Deer in the clearing?"

Before anyone could stop him, the marshal hobbled over to the door, opened it quickly, and jumped outside.

"You idiot!" Desmond groaned.

At the sound of the cabin door opening, the deer went off like rockets. White flaggy tails flashed and lean compressed bodies sprang into bounding hops. It was as though the five animals were a hand grenade that had just exploded into five separate pieces. Annie looked across the clearing and into a wall of tree trunks. The deer had gone without a sound, silently bounding away through all the young timber and undergrowth as though they had never existed. For a moment Annie wondered if she had actually seen those five sleek animals.

"They're gone." She turned to Desmond.

The marshal came limping back inside the hut. "What happened? I didn't even see them."

Desmond shook his head in disgust. "How could you, for pete's sake! You went blundering out there like an army tank."

141 __

The marshal bristled with anger. "I tell you I didn't *see* any deer. Did you see any?"

"Well no," Desmond had to admit.

"So maybe there weren't any. Maybe Annie imagined them."

"Did you really see deer?" Mr. Lusty asked.

"Yes. Five or six of them and two of them were small, just babies," Annie said.

Desmond began to have his doubts. They were all so weak now from loss of food that they tended to spend hours just slumped on the floor, daydreaming. Perhaps those deer had been the tail end of Annie's daydream, an image carried over into real life.

"I tell you, I *saw* them," Annie insisted.

"Yes, sure you saw them," Desmond said. It would be easy to find out, he thought. If there were as many as Annie said, surely one of them would have left some tracks out in the clearing? He got to his feet and took a deep breath to test that pain in his side. The soreness was still there and he still felt lightheaded but at least that awful hacking cough had left him for a while. And there had been no more blood since the night before. Slowly he made his way to the door. "I'm going out for a minute," he said.

No one answered. Taking plenty of time Desmond walked to the middle of the clearing to look for tracks. He found none in the hard frozen ground but began to work out in circles from the center and soon found what he was looking for, two separate shaped pads with

— 142

pointed front ends. The front edges of the tracks were heavily embedded, the back ends just barely visible, a sign that the animal had made the imprint on landing from a jump. He soon found other tracks and, a further piece of indisputable evidence, a small mound of brown pellets still faintly steaming.

While he was at it, he checked out the snares and found them empty. Bringing a handful of loose branches with him, he re-entered the cabin and dropped the firewood in the fuel corner. "Annie was right," he said. "The clearing is full of deer tracks. Even fresh manure."

"Well, I couldn't shoot what I couldn't see," the marshal said. "And I can hardly move with this hip."

"The way you went crashing out there, you made sure there wasn't going to be anything to see," Desmond said. Suddenly he felt weak and eased himself down until he was sitting on the floor again. His face tightened into a grimace as pain once again stabbed his side. Surely that cough wasn't coming back?

"Desmond, you're not making sense," Annie said. "The marshal didn't deliberately scare away the deer."

"No, he was just stupid was all."

"Please everybody, calm down," Mr. Lusty said. "All this bickering will get us nowhere." The old man cast an appealing glance over at Annie.

Annie lifted the water bowl from the table. "We're practically out of water," she said. "Desmond, could you manage to get us more water?"

Hunched over, one hand to his side, Desmond lifted his head long enough to say, "I'm too sick, Annie. I'm sorry."

"We need more wood, too," the marshal said, then glared across at Desmond. "That little handful you brought in isn't going to last very long."

"Why don't *you* go and get some," Annie said. "I can't do everything. I've never seen such a selfish bunch of people." She left the cabin, carrying the water bowl.

Desmond cradled his head on his drawn-up knees and tried to keep the pain away. It was hopeless, they were never going to get rescued. Across from him, the marshal picked up a pack of cards and began to lay out a new game of Patience.

Old Mr. Lusty retrieved the legal pad from the briefcase and prepared to write another entry in his journal. This was by far the worst day yet for fighting and backbiting. He didn't think they could take another day like it.

18

John dozed in front of his fire. Like some instant replay that he could not turn off, he kept re-living the crash. And no matter how many times he ran the scene, something was still missing. Two men had gone up the aisle to the bathroom. One man put his hand on the seat in front of John. That hand had a red mark across the wrist, the marshal's hand. Then the two men talked to the stewardess. Then the three people were no longer in sight. Some loud noises from the front of the plane. Maybe five minutes later he looked out the window. Just about then a man came hurrying back down the aisle. John saw trees, a mountain, then the crash. Panicsville. A blow on the head, a coat over his eyes, the safety belt, helping Mr. Lusty and then the wounded man, the hijacker, out of the wreck. Something still missing. What was it? The man going up the aisle.

Hand on the seat. The marshal's hand, no, not the marshal's hand. Marshal O'Connor was still in his seat in the back. Had to be the other detective's hand. Or the hijacker's hand. Of course, the hijacker's hand. The mark was the mark of handcuffs. Quite simple. Marshal had the same mark. Because he and the prisoner had been handcuffed together. And when the prisoner said he had to go to the bathroom, the two cops had uncuffed him. Yes, all very clear. Prisoner was probably handcuffed on each side to a detective. Funny he hadn't seen the cuffs when he looked back at the three men. No, the prisoner wasn't handcuffed that way because the marshal had been sitting in the middle. He clearly remembered now the face of the marshal in between the other two. And the marshal didn't know what "ten-four" meant, he had called it gibberish. He had called it gibberish because . . . Yes, now he had it, now it all fell into place. Marshal had cuff marks on *both* wrists. Had to be the other. The mystery was solved. He could go to sleep now and tell Mark later.

After a while a murmuring sound began to tease his mind. The low humming noise reminded him of standing on the iron gratings in the center of Broadway and 112th Street in New York City, the open gratings through which one could see the subway tracks and hear the underground rumble of an approaching train.

He opened his eyes and reality came flooding back. He was alone in the woods waiting beside a railroad track. He stood up and stretched his arms, then immediately sat down again to let the dizzy spell pass. A minute later, having regained his sense of balance, he got to his feet and threw several branches on the fire, sending a stream of sparks skyward. Then he hunkered down, cocked his knees out in a V, and spread his hands to the flames. There was a funny hum in his ears.

Suddenly he felt the earth move! A slight tremor ran through the ground under his feet. He held his breath and waited. Was there a train coming? The winds clashed through the tops of the trees, filling the night with the sound of their passage. It was hard to tell whether he was hearing the wind or some other noise.

Then he remembered something a friend had once told him. He went over and placed his hand on one of the rails. The cold steel stung his flesh but there, in the very tips of his fingers, he could feel the faint tremble of a vibration in the rail.

Quickly he jumped up and piled more wood on the fire. When the train came into view, he would step into the beam of the headlight and, between that and the fire, they would have to see him and stop the train.

He pulled a burning branch from the fire. The one he plucked had an end that was burning a bright cherry red. As soon as he saw the train he would wave the branch back and forth.

A minute later the sound of a train came from deep within the woods. The noise grew in volume and John checked his fire. It was blazing up very nicely now. He stepped across the rail, inside the tracks, and waited, holding up his burning branch.

It was very dark, with an overcast sky, so dark that he

147 __

could not see more than a few yards down the track. Now the rhythmic clicking of wheels was much louder and he thought he saw something black move in the shadows ahead of him. What was it? Where was the engine with its bright headlights? He began to wave his branch back and forth. Somewhere far ahead of him a white light flashed on, as though in answer to his wave. He waved again, guessing that the light was the head-light of an engine a couple of hundred feet down the track. But black shadows seemed to build, then tumble toward him, a voice shouted something, and he pan-icked, leaping clear of the rail and roadbed and falling to his knees. Almost immediately he heard the agoniz-ing screech of steel wheels trying to stop on steel rails. A light dropped from somewhere, two feet hit the cinders beside the roadbed, and a dark figure loomed over him.

"You all right?"

He looked up. Laden cars were trundling by, their wheels still locked and screeching. The dark figure turned away from him and began to swing a lantern slowly back and forth. "What happened?" the brake-man called back over his shoulder. "You get lost in the woods?"

John had to shout to be heard above the squeal of the wheels. "Yeah. I was on a plane that crashed."

The figure came over and shone the lantern in his eyes. "A plane crash?"

"Yeah, about two weeks ago. I got a buddy who's

— 148

hurt about two miles back in the woods. And about fifty miles further back there's four more in a cabin.''

The locomotive had now drawn abreast of him and stopped. It had been pushing thirty tip cars full of iron ore ahead of it. The railway was a private one belonging to a mine, and it ran some twenty miles between the mine and the smelter. The train pushed the full ore cars to the smelter, where they were tipped sideways and emptied. The brakeman normally rode on the front of the first loaded car on the evening run to the smelter.

''What's the problem, Al?'' the engineer called down.

The brakeman pushed John ahead of him up on the steel steps that led into the cab. The engineer reached down and pulled John inside. John sat down on a wooden box and explained the plane crash and his trek out for help. The engineer poured him a cup of tea from a thermos bottle and then gave him an orange, the only bit of food that either of the two trainmen had with them. John methodically peeled the fruit, then sank his teeth into the sweet pulp. He closed his eyes while he chewed, savoring the taste and texture of the orange.

''How long's it been since you've eaten?'' the engineer asked.

''Four or five days, maybe a week. I can't remember exactly, I lost track of the days.'' Then John surprised the two men, and especially himself, by starting to cry. For several minutes great tears rolled down his cheeks and fell to the steel floor of the cab. The engineer turned away and lifted a rag. He began to polish the already gleaming glass faces of a row of dials. Beside him, the brakeman, a toothpick in one corner of his mouth, stared out the window and into the dark. The two men waited for John to get control of himself. Then the engineer turned around and asked, "How long will it take to reach your friend?"

"About three hours, but it will take longer coming back because he's broken his ankle and can't walk."

The engineer checked his watch. "It's ten past nine now. Do you think he can stay where he is until morning?"

"Yes, he has a fire and everything."

"Because we can take you in to the smelter. From there we can phone the Mounties in Saint Jean and ask them to send in a rescue party. They won't want to go in tonight if they can help it. But they'll have everybody rounded up and ready to start at first light. Now we make our first run back to the mine at six A.M. and we can take them with us and drop them off here. They should reach your friend well before noon."

John shook his head in puzzlement. "Mounties? What Mounties?"

"Canadian Mounted Police. This is Canada."

"Canada?" John shook his head. "Wow, Canada! Hey, this is the first time I've been out of the United States. Well almost," he smiled to himself, remembering his imaginary trip with Mark.

The engineer laughed at John's reaction. "If you had

some grub in you, and a good night's sleep, could you join with the rescue party in the morning?''

"You better believe it.''

"Because I have a feeling they'll want you along.''

John patted his pocket. "We made a sort of map for them to follow.''

The engineer turned to his brakeman. "Okay Al, let's roll.''

The brakeman dropped from the cab. A couple of minutes later John looked through the window of the locomotive and saw, just beyond the last rounded carload of ore, a white light trace three or four rapid circles in the dark.

The locomotive jerked, slipped, jerked again, then slowly began to pick up speed.

As they approached the dying fire beside the tracks, John reached over and tugged the engineer's arm.

"Yeah?''

"Could you blow your whistle? Maybe my friend will hear it.''

The engineer gave a sudden understanding grin, then reached for the cord. The horn rent the night air, long blast after long blast, making the woods ring with sound for a solid couple of minutes.

"Hey, you guys,'' John called silently to all his friends, and especially to Mark alone in the woods beside his dying campfire. "Hey, you guys, we finally made it!''

19

Mark reached out, caught a stick of firewood, and heaved it onto the dying coals. He gave a shiver and tried to pull the blanket tighter around his shoulders. He was afraid of falling asleep and letting the fire go out. His trouble was that he was passing out from time to time. He had not wanted to say anything to John in case his friend thought it was a plea for him to stay behind. Anyway the weakness hadn't bothered him when he was on the move because the least little jiggle of his bad leg sent pain knifing through him, shocking him wide awake. But when he sat down, and made the bad leg comfortable, the first thing he knew everything got dark and blacked out on him. The big red heart of the fire got smaller and smaller until it was a tiny red dot, like the white dot in the middle of the screen when you switched off the TV set. And then even the red dot faded away and he could see nothing and hear nothing except a low buzzing sound in his ears.

The light faded from the sky and it grew dark. Somehow he had to get through the night. All he could do was concentrate on keeping the fire lit. John said that if he wasn't back before dark, it meant that he had reached someone. But Mark didn't put too much faith in that promise. Anything could happen. John could get lost and not be able to find his way back. Or he could decide to keep on going as long as he could and forget about Mark. Or overcome by weakness, unable to move another step, he might have crawled into some hole and waited to die. Mark sighed. The problem was he kept getting sleepier and sleepier, even dreaming that he was back home. He extended the fork with the white ball stuck on the end. He and his sister were toasting marshmallows in the barbecue fireplace in their backyard. Dad was at the hospital working late and Mom was at one of her political meetings. Two houses down some kids were playing basketball. He could hear the hollow thumping of the ball on concrete, the slight pinging noise of the ball hitting the rim, the shouts of the kids. He ate his brown melting marshmallow, then speared a fresh one. Somewhere far away a police siren started up. It got closer and closer, was evidently coming right up their street.

Mark's head jerked up in sudden fright. Where was he? What was that noise? The fire! Painfully he sat up. Train? Off in the woods the blast was repeated, three or four strident hoots. A train! It had to be! Again half a dozen long blasts. There was an urgency about the whistles that clearly indicated something out of the ordinary. They weren't the usual warnings blown for a grade crossing somewhere ahead. These whistles sounded like a message of some sort, even a celebration. Of course! They were signaling him, telling him that John had been picked up, telling him to be patient, not to lose heart, help was on the way.

Mark shook his head. He had to concentrate, to keep the fire going. The smoke would be a signal to them in the morning. Anyway he needed that fire to keep warm. He reached forward and poked in the heart of the ashes with a stick. The almost dead fire looked like a clock— with the unburned ends of sticks arranged in a circle, like the hour markers on a dial, around the white hub of ashes in the middle. Using the end of his crutch, Mark pushed and prodded unburned ends into the center where there was still a handful of hot coals lurking beneath a blanket of white ash. The wood began to smoke, then a tiny flame licked up.

Mark smiled. He had saved the fire. In a minute or two he would pile on some fresh firewood. So his buddy had made it. The question now was, would they try to find him tonight, or wait until morning? It really didn't make too much difference. By this time tomorrow night he would be in a hospital somewhere, getting his leg taken care of. And he needed that leg in good shape. He and John had a lot of cycling to do come summertime.

He threw half a dozen branches on the fire and tried to stay awake. Despite his best intentions, he nodded off from time to time, but each time he did so the fire got low, his bad leg got cold and began to hurt, and he woke up in time to get the fire going again.

The last time he fell asleep it was early morning and he never did see the six men come out of the trees and follow the stream down to his fire. One of the men had to shake him awake and when Mark finally opened his eyes, it was to see the beautiful red-bearded face of a young giant beaming down at him.

"Good to see you," Mark said weakly, then grinned. "Did my buddy, John, send you?"

"That's right. You're okay now. Your friend said to tell you that he was going back to the cabin."

"To the cabin?"

"He said he had some unfinished business to take care of. Now, let's take a look at that ankle of yours."

20

Annie came in from the early morning cold, went to the fire, and spread her hands. She had been out checking the snares. The others were lying in their accustomed spots in front of the fireplace.

Desmond sat up, pulled a blanket around his shoulders, and shivered. "Nothing?"

"No."

Annie looked at the other two. Old Mr. Lusty was in bad shape. For the past two days he had had to be helped to his feet by either Annie or the marshal and then supported on his short trips outside the cabin.

Marshal O'Connor was bearing up a little better. His face still had a little color and though he could barely walk more than a few feet before his hip joint gave out, it had spared him from the more strenuous jobs of gathering wood and water.

Annie sat down beside Desmond. "How do you feel?"

Desmond shook his head. "Not very good."

The marshal pushed a stick of wood into the fire. "I think one of you kids ought to go back to the wreck."

Annie groaned. "We've been over this before."

"Maybe one of you could work down to the front of the plane and find some food," the marshal said.

"We'd never make it. Besides, animals or birds will have gotten whatever food might have survived the fire," Annie argued.

Desmond lifted his head. "Sssh, sssh, what's that?"

Marshal O'Connor sat up.

"That noise, it's a plane!"

Annie jumped to her feet and opened the cabin door. Behind her hobbled O'Connor.

"There it is!" she yelled as a small blue and white plane came soaring out from behind a range of clouds, sailed over the clearing, then rose and banked for a turn. Five minutes later, as the plane came over on a second run, Desmond had the fire sending up dense clouds of white smoke.

Annie was dancing around outside, flashing the mirror, waving her arms, and screaming with joy. The plane disappeared but minutes later came into view once more on its third and final run over the clearing. The plane dipped to within five hundred feet of ground level, then rose, banked, and cleared a nearby mountain ridge. The sound of the motor grew fainter and fainter, until finally the cone of sound reached the vanishing point and stillness reigned once more.

Annie threw out her arms and appealed to O'Connor. "He saw us, didn't he? He *had* to!"

"I don't know, I just don't know," the marshal said, turning away.

"Why didn't he waggle his wings or something?" Annie cried. "Why didn't he give some sign that he saw us?"

"I don't know, I just don't know," the marshal shook his head.

Annie headed back to the cabin. A few steps from the door she turned to look back. The sky was black behind the nearby mountain ridge. Even as she watched, the area of blackness grew and grew, spreading over the clearing until the wall of blackness was everywhere and nothing could be seen and night covered everything. Then the next thing she knew she was falling.

When she opened her eyes again it was dark. Someone had let the fire go out. "Desmond?" she called. "Mr. Lusty?"

"I'm right here, child," the old man said.

"Why is it so dark, who let the fire go out?"

"It's all right, don't worry." Mr. Lusty glanced over at the marshal and Desmond. It was broad daylight. In fact only ten minutes or so had passed since the marshal, Desmond, and Mr. Lusty between them had somehow managed to half drag, half carry Annie back inside the cabin.

But Annie had already guessed what was wrong. "I

can't see. It's daylight, isn't it?" she cried. She put her two hands up in front of her face. "I can't even see my *hands!*"

"I'm sure it's only temporary," Mr. Lusty said.

"And the plane, it didn't come back?" she asked.

No one answered.

"Oh God!" she cried out. "It's all over!"

Annie was now openly crying.

"I'm sure it's only temporary," Mr. Lusty kept saying over and over. "I'm sure it comes from that blow you took on your nose. Probably when you fell you re-injured the same place. I've heard of cases like that before, it usually clears up in a day or so."

"Sure," Desmond said. He put one arm around Annie's shoulders. "I read where it happened to a racing driver once, he was blind for three days but then he got his sight back completely."

"It will clear up," Mr. Lusty promised. "It can't be anything too serious, Annie."

Annie patted the floor in front of her knees. "Where did I put the mirror?"

"Oh God, what's the use?" the marshal said. "Whatever happens now we're not going to . . ."

But whatever the marshal was going to say was drowned out by the steadily rising sound of an airplane engine.

"He's coming back!" Annie screamed.

Helping each other, somehow all four got to their feet and staggered outside. Desmond guided Annie as the others watched the plane make another run over the clearing. This time a dark object fell from the fuselage and tumbled end over end. It came plummeting down and landed almost dead center in the middle of the clearing.

"What's happening?" Annie cried, her face lifted to the sky.

Desmond reached the square cardboard box first. The package had burst open on impact but whoever had packed the food knew his job. The box had been lined inside with loaves of bread. Inside the lining of loaves there were candy bars and tins of fish and meat. Someone had thoughtfully taped a can opener to the inside of the box.

"It's food, it's food, Annie," Desmond cried. "The plane dropped a box of food." He began unloading the contents into the trembling hands of O'Connor and Mr. Lusty.

"Show me," Annie cried, and Desmond tucked a loaf of bread in her arms and guided her back inside the cabin.

The food rejuvenated them all. There was a can of tuna fish, a can of sardines, a can of salmon, a can of beef stew, a can of meatballs, a can of cooked Viennese sausage, and eight candy bars—two for each person.

Desmond opened several cans and he and the marshal began making sandwiches. Desmond brought a sandwich over to Annie. "Here, this is tuna fish, Annie." Then he brought another to Mr. Lusty. He helped the old man sit up, then placed the sandwich in his trembling hands.

— 160

"You see," Mr. Lusty feebly said. "I told you all not to give way . . ."

"To despair," Desmond smiled and finished for him.

The old man took a bite of the sandwich, chewed a minute or so, and then said, "I was just getting used to not eating."

"It's strange, but I'm not very hungry at all." Desmond ate half a sandwich and one of the chocolate bars, but that was all he could manage. Just the act of swallowing hurt his throat and chest too much. The marshal and Annie ate two sandwiches apiece and it was decided to save the remaining food until later. They were still not sure when or how they would be rescued. For all they knew it might be another day or two before anyone could reach them.

It was mid-afternoon before they had their answer, the heavy pulsing swoosh of chopper blades in the distance. The helicopter hovered high above them for a while, then slid sideways and crabbed back and forth as it lost altitude. Finally it settled softly on its skids in the middle of the clearing, flattening the grass all around. On one side of the plane were the words, "Canadian Air Force."

A man dressed in Canadian Air Force uniform and carrying a blue flight bag stepped down from the machine and, running in a crouch, came toward them.

"I'm Captain McLean," he said. "I'm a doctor."

Before anyone could answer, Desmond spotted the tall young black emerging from the aircraft, followed by a Canadian Mountie.

"John!" Desmond called. "Hey everybody, John's here!"

In a moment John was being embraced by Desmond and then Annie.

"Hey what happened to you?" John said to Annie, noting the strange vacant stare she was giving him.

"I can't see. Something happened to my eyes."

"Well, it'll be all right, now. You'll be out of here and getting medical help before you know it."

"But where's Mark? Is he with you?" Annie asked.

"He's fine, except for an ankle that's being taken care of right now." Then John turned quickly and pointed to Marshal O'Connor, who had begun to move toward the helicopter. "That's him," John said to the Mountie. "That's the real hijacker."

The Mountie started to say something but suddenly Marshal O'Connor had his gun out and was pointing it at both the Mountie and the pilot who had stepped out of the copter. "Listen you, I'm very sick and you've got to fly me out first," he said to the pilot. "I'm a police officer and that's an order! You can come back later for the others."

"Now take it easy." The pilot began to back away.

But John was already in the air in a diving tackle that caught O'Connor around the knees and brought him crashing to the ground. The marshal was no match for a rested and rejuvenated John. Soon the younger man was handing the gun to the Mountie and saying, "You better put cuffs on him."

"What's this all about?" Mr. Lusty asked.

"He's no marshal, he's the hijacker," John said.

"The hijacker!" Mr. Lusty and Annie said in unison.

"The real marshal died the night of the crash. His body's back there with the plane," John said.

"You're crazy!" the marshal shouted. He appealed to the Mountie. "That kid got hit on the head during the crash and it's affected him. I'm Marshal O'Connor. There's a wallet in my pocket. Take it out and you'll find all my identification."

The Mountie extracted the wallet. There were a dozen I.D. cards of one sort or another, all issued to James O'Connor.

"He's right, you know," the Mountie said to John.

John came over. "Let's see those cards for a moment." He riffled through them, found one with the date of birth on it. "What's your date of birth?" he asked.

"I . . . uh . . . it's, I'm sorry. This crash must have affected my memory," the marshal blustered.

John found a small photograph of a pretty young woman and two children standing in front of a body of water. He held the photograph in front of the marshal. "Where was this photograph taken?"

"At a lake."

"What's the name of the lake?"

"I can't remember."

"Is it Moose Lake?" John prompted.

"Yes, that's it, Moose Lake."

"And it was taken when?"

"I can't remember. In the summer."

"Was it July fourth?"

"Yes, yes, I think it was. That's right, our Fourth of July picnic."

John showed the back of the photo to the Mountie. On it was written, "Bear Lake. August 3, 1973."

"You'll have a chance to prove your innocence when we reach Saint Jean," the Mountie said. He put a pair of handcuffs on his prisoner and pushed him ahead and up into the chopper.

"I can't believe it," Annie exclaimed. "You know, I felt something was wrong, right at the start. But how did you figure it out, John?"

"Bunch of little things fell into place. I remembered looking back at the three men in the rear seat of the plane." John motioned to the chopper. "He, the so-called marshal, was sitting in the *middle*. It didn't strike me until much later but the normal place for a prisoner would be between his two escorts. Then the first night after the crash the real marshal, just before he died, said a couple of things when his mind was wandering. He said his lawn mower was on the fritz and he used the expression, 'ten-four.' "

"Yes, I remember that," Mr. Lusty said.

"Well, 'ten-four' is a police term and when someone asked what it meant, that guy said it was gibberish. If he were a real marshal he would have known what 'ten-four' meant. And anyway, what kind of a bank robber would be talking about his lawn mower?"

"You're right," Annie nodded.

"The other thing that bothered me was him saying he hadn't seen anyone come back down the aisle just before the plane crashed. I saw somebody, how could *he* have missed him? Because he didn't see him. He, the hijacker, was the person coming down the aisle. And right after the crash I noticed, when he was helping me get stuff into the cabin, that he had red marks on both his wrists. The real marshal would have had red cuff marks on only one wrist."

The Mountie returned, holding the marshal's gun. "Did you know his gun was empty?"

"No," John said.

"No bullets in his gun?" Annie shook her head. "No wonder he never got anything when he went hunting. It all fits in!" she exclaimed. "And he was afraid of anyone else using the gun, because if we found out it was empty, he wouldn't be able to bluff whoever came to rescue us."

"But where are the bullets?" Mr. Lusty asked.

"The real marshal must have hid them somewhere, when he handed over his gun to the stewardess," John said.

"And that's the reason he blundered out and scared those deer in the clearing," Desmond joined in, buttoning up his jacket as the doctor finished his examination. "I knew that was deliberate!"

"Take it easy now, young man," the doctor said. "You may well have pneumonia, but I think we got to you in time. Now, young lady, let's take a look at you."

While Annie's eyes were being looked at, John told them about how he and Mark had managed, about the bear, the porcupine, Mark's fall, and finally the train

165 __

tracks . . . "I was sitting there by the fire waiting for a train to come by . . . sort of dozing, when suddenly. . . ."

"Hate to break this up," the pilot called. "But we better be getting back now."

"Yes," the Mountie said. "Daylight permitting, we should make another trip back in here as soon as possible to check the crash site and the dead man."

Taking Annie by the arm, John guided her over and up into the chopper, where he placed her in a seat beside Desmond. Then he went back to help the Mountie and the pilot lift Mr. Lusty into the craft.

Soon the chopper was rising from the clearing. John had one last glimpse of the old cabin roof before the chopper side-slipped away over the ridgeline.

21

The two young men sat at a plain wooden table in a youth hostel in Yorkshire and glumly looked out the window at the driving rain that showed no signs of slacking off.

"Another day with nothing to do," John said.

Mark grunted. "No sense in trying to go out in that downpour."

"I suppose not," John agreed. "Whatever happened to all that lovely sparkling English sunshine we're supposed to be pedaling through? This is the third day we've been stuck here."

"At least my ankle is getting a good rest," Mark said. "Hey, let's get out that map and plot our route up to Scotland."

"Naw, we already done that a couple of times. I got a better idea. Why don't we read that letter again?"

"Annie's letter?"

"Yeah."

Mark went over to his pack and fished out the letter he had received a few days before in Leeds, at the General Delivery window. He opened it and began to read, "Dear Mark and John." He lowered the letter. "You'll notice that she put me first."

"Right on, dirt always goes before the broom."

"I hope you guys are having a good time," Mark continued reading. "All kinds of things are happening here. My eyes are all better. The doctors say there was no physical reason for my blindness and that it was all psychological. They say it happened because I couldn't face going in and telling everybody the plane hadn't seen us again. 'Hysterical blindness' they called it. How do you like that? Anyway I'm back to normal. And we had to give evidence again. Mr. Lusty has been on a couple of TV shows. He was kind of cute. He kept saying, 'All the credit belongs to the young folks, they never gave way to despair.' The hijacker is still awaiting trial. You guys better get back here soon, cause we're all going to have to testify. Desmond is all better now. In fact he and I have been out on a couple of dates. You won't believe this but we went to see a movie called, 'Skyjacked!' Desmond says that the whole experience has changed him. Can you believe this? He now wants to go to Forestry School and become a forest ranger. Oh and I nearly forgot. Down-East Airways has donated five thousand dollars to a scholarship fund for the four of us. Livingstone College has already received the money. Have fun, you guys. See you soon. Hugs and kisses.''

"Well, that killed a good two minutes," John said. "Now what do we do?"

Mark laughed.

"Tell you what," John went on. "Let's pretend we're on an airliner that has just been hijacked and it's about to crash deep in the Canadian woods.''

"And we're sitting in the back of the plane, right?"

"Right on, man."

But John couldn't keep it up and he began to laugh. Mark joined him and the kitchen of the youth hostel rang with their laughter. Within minutes they were doubled over the kitchen table, trying to stop, gasping for breath as they helplessly laughed on, tears streaming from their eyes.

Two Tunisian students entered the kitchen, looked at the two of them, then turned to each other and grinned.

"How do you say in English, they are crazy?" asked one.

The other nodded and with his forefinger traced a small circle over his temple. "Oh yes, crazy Americans," he agreed.

ABOUT THE AUTHOR

Arthur Roth was born in New York City. He received his B.A. from Arizona State University and his M.A. from Columbia University. He is the author of *The Iceberg Hermit* and *Snowbound*. He lives in Amagansett, New York.